Where Moonflowers Dance

J. Laura Chandler

WOODBRIDGE
PUBLISHERS

276 5th Avenue Suite 704 #944

New York, NY 10001

Copyright © 2025 J. Laura Chandler

ISBN (Paperback) : 978-1-917760-68-3

ISBN (Hardback) : 978-1-917760-69-0

ISBN (eBook) : 978-1-917760-70-6

All rights reserved

This novel is entirely a work of fiction. The names, characters and incidents portrayed in it are the work of the author's own imagination. Any resemblance to actual persons, living or dead, locations or events is purely coincidental.
No part of this publication may be reproduced, stored in a retrieval system, copied in any form or by any means, electronic, mechanical, photocopying, recording or otherwise transmitted without written permission from the publisher. You must not circulate this book in any format.

Cover Design by Woodbridge Publishers

This novel is dedicated to Chloe Belle and Kenadee.

I admire both of you for walking in God's confidence. I'm thankful you both are using your creative and artistic talent, and I hope that one day, you'll have a deep appreciation for growing things in the soil like my parents did. Both of you girls have many characteristics of Mom and Dad…they live on through you. Always loving you and praying that you wait on the Lord for Him to choose your life's mate.

Somehow, I know you will.

Introduction

Early morning had always been her favorite time of day. She cherished each morning with her first cup of coffee as one of the richest treasures her heart and taste buds could embrace. The melodious sounds of gulls overhead combined with lapping waves spoke to her soul of eternity and her deep desire to see her loved ones who had departed.

She shielded her eyes from the sun and looked in the direction he would be walking at the ocean's edge, where the sand glistened, and little sea creatures frantically scooted on the surface when the waves rhythmically retreated to the deep. No sign of him yet.

He had no idea she was looking for him. She did not think he knew she existed but was confident their paths would cross in time. For more than two weeks now, she had spent every morning watching him walk on the sand alone. He always dressed the same: casual white trousers, a white shirt, and a straw hat that halfway shielded his face from the sun. His gait was graceful and unhurried.

Just last night, she had dreamed about being with him. He had lightly touched her when they first met, and she had reached out and placed her hand on his. A small gesture, and yet, recalling their initial connection in her dream, stirred the deep chords of her heart and awakened longing for another. Longing for *him*. Thinking about a spiritual and physical connection filled her with expectancy and hope.

She felt the wind pick up, and suddenly, her hat had blown several feet away. After trailing it for a good while and finally collecting it, as well as herself, she looked once again for any sign of him before walking back to her bungalow.

Chapter One

Gwenyth Ray Belltower, known as Ray by her beloved family and friends, had left the States and moved to the small island of Grand Cayman two years earlier. Ray lived modestly but comfortably. She had been fortunate enough to purchase a run-down cottage before it went on the market and, during the last two years, had restored it with the help of a contractor in the community.

Most of the backyard was designated for her garden. It had taken her six months to prepare the soil with wood chips, compost, and peat. She loved every minute of the preparation. The rhythmic labor of turning the soil, feeling the earth between her fingers, and watching tiny green sprouts push through had been a healing process in itself. This little piece of land had become her sanctuary.

Her contractor, Saxton, was well-known in the community. He had moved to the island when he was a young man and never left. His connections and advice had enabled

Ray to become familiar with the island folk. Since Cayman was mainly a tourist attraction, the core of locals was guarded and very private. Ray felt blessed that Saxton had introduced her to a group of supportive friends.

The weather forecast for the day was sunny and 72 degrees. Ray showered, dressed, and slipped on walking shoes. A quaint strip mall with boutiques, side-walk cafes, and a small grocery store was located less than a mile away. She wanted to mingle and, perhaps, bump into the mystery man who had piqued her curiosity. A stranger she had glimpsed in passing, always just out of reach, a fleeting presence in the background of her days.

The birds created a lovely symphony for her enjoyment, and today was one of those days when her body felt agile and alive. She couldn't help but long for serendipity to be sprinkled along her path.

As she slowed her pace, she felt a presence brush against her thigh. Startled but not alarmed, she looked down to discover a gorgeous, mahogany red retriever walking along beside her.

Ray said, "Hey buddy, are you lost?" as she gently rubbed his head and across his back. His coat was like satin, and she couldn't help but marvel at the beauty of this creature.

"Say, let me check your neck." No collar. "Where do you live, little fella?"

All she got as an answer was a nudge of his head into her hands, a silent plea for more pets.

As she continued her walk towards town, the dog remained close to her side. She remembered a veterinary clinic located close to the strip mall and thought it a good idea to take the dog there, hoping someone might recognize him.

As she opened the clinic door, she saw no one waiting and felt more comfortable letting the dog enter with no leash.

A receptionist smiled and said, "How can we help you?"

Ray explained the situation and asked that the dog be examined for an identification chip. After a thorough vet examination with no luck finding a chip, Ray placed her number on the lost and found board and purchased a collar, harness, leash, and bag of kibble for her new buddy.

Going to town was for another time, she needed to return home with her new pet and bag of goodies. As she strolled along, she observed carefully the properties on both sides of the road, but did not notice anyone out and about or calling for their dog. When she arrived home and opened the little front gate, her newfound friend seemed excited. Perhaps he knew this would be his new home.

Ray stretched and yawned. She and her new buddy slept much later than she customarily did. It felt absolutely marvelous.

"What are we going to name you? I'm not sure, but I don't think 'hey you' would be appropriate. You and I are on a new journey, aren't we? How about the name 'Journey?'"

Journey stretched his back legs behind him and stared at her.

Ray said, "Settled then. Your new name is Journey. Are you hungry, Journey?"

He leaped off the bed and headed to the kitchen.

"Oh my goodness, he understands English! Guess we've got a man in a dog suit!"

She trailed behind him and turned on the coffee maker. "This morning, we are having bacon and pancakes. After you eat your kibble, I'll let you sample a little bacon!" It felt good to have something else, another soul, to talk with. A new place can feel pretty lonely and Ray was glad she'd met Journey.

Ray was fond of her small courtyard, where she had a table and two chairs. A small koi pool separated the patio from the garden area. In the back part of the property was a wooden fence with moonflower vines planted three feet apart. In another month, the vines would completely take over. She looked forward to sitting on the patio in the evening when the moonflowers would unfold. During a full moon, the flowers looked like iridescent saucers. Their fragrance was faint but heavenly, and in the evenings, when the ocean breeze was pronounced, the moonflower blossoms would move in circular motions and remind one of the angels dancing in the wind, a sight that never failed to fill her with wonder.

Ray laughed at herself, for sometimes, the combination of her imagination and soul's desire for the heavenly realm both amazed and amused her.

As she finished the last bite of a pancake, she heard Journey growl. She stood up and walked into the house. Rarely did she have guests, but someone was knocking on her front door.

To her surprise, there he stood as she gently opened the door. Journey whined and greeted him with excitement.

"Hello. My name is Blake Forsyth. I've found my dog, as you can see!"

Ray exclaimed. "It is obvious he has missed you! Please come in."

Blake cautiously stepped in and tried to apologize for the intrusion. Journey did not give either of them a chance to converse or properly make introductions.

"Mr. Forsyth, would you like a cup of coffee?" Ray asked.

"Yes, that would be lovely."

"It is pleasant outside this morning, so why don't you enjoy the patio area while I get some coffee and scones for us."

When Blake walked out in the backyard, he was taken aback at how well put together everything was. Enchanting would perhaps better describe the charming area. The smells of herbs and fresh earth delighted his senses. The little cottage seemed alive and inviting.

Ray set a tray on the small table and motioned for Blake to have a seat.

Blake smiled and put a hand out to stroke Journey.

Ray announced, "Your dog has a new name, and he seems to respond well to it."

Blake asked, "And what would that name be?"

"Journey."

"Perhaps Journey should be his name now. I gave little thought to his name and had decided to just call him 'Red' because of his coloring."

"Oh my, how could I forget? I didn't get the chance to introduce myself. Mr. Forsyth, my name is Gwenyth Ray Belltower, but I go by Ray."

"Well, Ray, it is, but only if you call me Blake. I cannot be much older than you, so no 'mister' please!"

"I'll work on it! Now, please enjoy your coffee and blueberry scones. The scones were made yesterday morning before I met Journey. I'm sure they are still fresh enough."

Blake nodded, taking a bite. The burst of sweetness, mixed with the flaky warmth of the pastry, was unexpectedly comforting.

"Delicious. Where did you get the blueberries?"

"There are two bushes by the back fence next to the moonflower vines."

"I did not notice the vines. Moonflowers were my mother's favorite!"

"They were my mother's favorite, too!" Ray happily added.

"May I ask what brings you to this beautiful little island?" Blake inquired.

"Many things, but for starters, the climate and beauty of the water and sand. Before moving here, I researched the locals and discovered that the community was cautious but friendly. I've found that to be true. Since there are so many tourists, the locals are relatively private yet kind and helpful. How about you? Do you live here? Or just vacationing?"

"I've leased a little villa here for the past few summers."

"I've learned that the winters are just as pleasant here," Ray commented.

"Well, it is always possible that I extend my stay!"

Journey whined and placed his head in Blake's lap, his big eyes looking up at him expectantly.

Ray asked, "Do you think he wants to go for a walk?"

"Perhaps. Would you like to join us? I'm sure Journey would love that. And well, I could use the company too."

"Of course. But I've just realized I'm barefoot. Give me a couple of minutes and I'll be back with some walking shoes."

Ray disappeared into the cottage, leaving Blake alone with Journey for a brief moment. The dog shifted his weight, his warm eyes watching Blake with an almost knowing expression. Blake absently stroked Journey's fur, his thoughts drifting.

The moonflowers. His mother. The mention of them had stirred something deep within him—a memory of her tending to her garden in the soft light of a summer evening, her hands delicate yet strong, guiding the blossoms to bloom. He hadn't thought about that in years.

Blake inhaled deeply, taking in the mingling scents of herbs and the sea air. The small island had already begun to weave its spell around him. There was something comforting here, something familiar yet unspoken, as though the universe had led him to this very moment.

When Ray returned, shoes on and a light shawl draped over her shoulders, she smiled warmly. "Shall we?"

Blake nodded, standing and letting Journey lead the way toward the winding garden path. For the first time in years, he felt a flicker of peace, as though he had finally stumbled upon a place where he could slow down, breathe, and perhaps even begin to heal.

Chapter Two

She felt the sun's warmth on her face and turned over to discover Journey was sleeping with her. Some nights, she left her window open, and since there were no screens, Journey must have jumped in and made himself at home.

"Oh my goodness, Journey, what will your owner think?" She chuckled, rubbing the dog's velvety ears before reaching for her phone. She searched for Blake's name in her phone, having exchanged numbers on their walk yesterday. Blake picked up on the second ring, his smooth voice calm from the other end.

"Good morning, Ray. I'm sure you want me to come get our dog."

"I suppose you are correct: he is now our dog. But no need to rush over. I have food for him, and if I hurry, he can accompany me on a run on the beach before it gets too late in the day for pets to be allowed. You know where he is, so feel free to wait until later when it is convenient for you."

"Thanks, Ray. I'll do just that. See you two later. Goodbye."

"Journey, what are we to do with you? Come to the kitchen, and I'll get you a bowl of food."

Ray changed clothes and prepared a protein drink with fresh mangoes and blueberries for herself. The vibrant colors of the fruit reminded her of the island's beauty, the way life here seemed to hum with a rhythm all its own.

Ray couldn't help but think back to her morning with Blake the day before. She did not question him, and he did not ask about anything concerning her personal life. They had romped on the beach like kids, looking for unique shells, while Journey ran circles around them. There had been a relaxed and comfortable silence between them. She knew her spirit was drawn to him. He was a beautiful man in every way, yet somewhat of a mystery. However, she found herself able to trust him. That in itself was unusual. Trust didn't come easily to her, yet with Blake, it felt natural.

She wondered about many things but would not bombard him with questions. For some reason, she felt too much information could take away from the joy in the moment.

"Come on, Journey, let's see what today unfolds for us."

After they had run at least a mile on the beach, Ray sat down on a knoll of dry sand and pulled Journey in beside her. Her thoughts went to a verse in the Bible: "No eye has seen, no ear has heard, no mind has conceived what God has prepared for those who love Him." *God Almighty, how I trust You and depend on You to light my path and allow me to be free in the peace You provide. I am thankful for Your Presence. I request this day to know Your wisdom and feel Your love in the path You have allowed me to walk.*

Ray's past was certainly a diverse one. She had very humble beginnings full of unknowns, but from the view and design of the divine One, her life had been filled with miracles laced throughout every passage.

Ray's birth mother was a teenager who died in the hospital from a suspected meth overdose shortly after delivering her. After extensive inquiries were made about her mother's identity with no luck, the authorities dismissed further investigation. Ray stayed in the hospital's care for two weeks after being born. Before social services were able to find an appropriate foster family, the ER doctor who delivered Ray volunteered to adopt her. He was in his early sixties and approaching retirement. His wife was in her late fifties. They had never been able to have children, so both of them desired to give this innocent baby a good start in life.

Dr. Belltower was fully aware of the health challenges that could unfold with the child because of the mother's addictions. He and his wife were more than willing to contribute their efforts and money to ensure the child had a decent life.

At times in Ray's life, she had wondered if a biological family member might try to locate her. Certainly, an inquiry could be made through medical records or even the adoption process. After adopting Byron, though, she no longer gave much thought to a possible connection with her biological family. She had the fondest memories of her adoptive parents, and they had encouraged her to become her own person - the individual that God had created her to be. She was made in the image of God, and that's the identity she felt comfortable with. Perhaps her adoption led her to want to give Byron a good life like she had been given: a way of paying it forward.

Blake was sitting in a rocker on the cottage's front porch, the rhythmic creak blending with the gentle rustle of the ocean breeze, when Ray and Journey returned.

Ray waved at him. "Good morning. Have you lost your dog again?" she joked.

"Yes. I think he likes you more than he likes me."

Journey darted ahead, tail wagging furiously, before leaping onto Blake's lap with an excited bark. It was obvious how much the dog loved him, but Ray noticed the subtle ease with which Journey alternated his affection between them as if trying to bridge two worlds.

Ray tilted her head, "What do you think made him come to my house during the night?"

"Maybe he is trying to give us the message that he wants to be with both of us."

"How about joint custody?"

"Now, that may work. I need to make a quick trip to Aberdeen, Scotland, and it seems Journey has already chosen you as his trusted guardian while I'm away."

Ray crossed her arms, feigning indignation, "I'm not sure I heard you ask me if it would be okay for him to stay with me!"

Blake held up his hands, a playful glint in his eye. "Ray, you are right. Sometimes, I assume too much. Please forgive me."

Ray let her smile grow. "I don't mind. When are you leaving?"

"I would like to depart in a couple of days. How does that sound?"

"I'd be happy to keep Journey," Ray said, glancing down at the dog now sprawled at her feet. "Though I must warn you he may never want to leave."

"I'll take my chances. Thank you so much, Ray. It means a lot to me."

She thought for a moment, and then her face lit up. "I've got an idea: stay for lunch. It won't take long for me to prepare a meal of fresh herbs and veggies from the garden. Sound good?"

"Yes. It sounds amazing. What can I do to help?"

"Absolutely nothing. You and Journey enjoy the weather on the patio while I dash to the garden and gather a few things. Give me thirty minutes, and you'll have the best meal you've had all week."

As Ray busied herself, Blake leaned back, watching the play of light through the trees and listening to the distant waves. The moment felt oddly perfect—unrushed, peaceful, like the island had been waiting for him to arrive at this very spot. Journey dozed by his feet, and for the first time in a long while, Blake felt something stir in his chest—a sense of home.

Lunch was a feast of fresh herbs, vibrant greens, and sun-warmed tomatoes. Afterwards, Ray brought two lounge chairs to the patio area and set them up where branches shaded them until the breeze picked up and sun rays filtered through the leaves of the low branches. Both Ray and Blake shared snippets of their earlier lives, and both were honest and transparent.

Ray opened up first, her voice steady yet tinged with vulnerability. She spoke of her Peace Corps tours right out of college, and after her parents passed, she used some of her inheritance funds to travel extensively in Europe. She also mentioned that she had adopted a thirteen-year-old boy named Byron in Latvia. But of course, all of this was ancient history, and her life had totally changed. Still, there were moments when she missed the version of herself that had roamed the world so freely.

Blake listened intently, his eyes never leaving her face. He noticed the pride in her words but also a quiet sorrow that she didn't dwell on.

When it was his turn, he shared pieces of his own story—the ache of his failed marriage, the bittersweet joy of watching his daughter grow up, and the fulfillment he'd found in his career as a fine art consultant.

After conversing for a couple of hours, Blake and Journey walked back to their house. Ray watched them go, pondering many things and feeling drawn to him. It was more than sexual attraction. It was a connection of their spirits, and she knew that he felt the same way. She couldn't help wondering where all this was going, her heart thrumming with something unfamiliar—hope.

Chapter Three

Blake's home base had been Glasgow, Scotland, for twenty years. After his wife divorced him, he had little desire for another relationship. Love had seemed like an unnecessary complication, something best left in the past. All his focus was now on his work.

Sadly, he did not share a healthy relationship with his daughter, Rachel, until she had started college. He had asked her to stay in Scotland and attend the University of Glasgow while her mother moved to America to chase her own dreams.

When Rachel graduated, she moved to America to be close to her mother. At that point, he had moved to Fraserburgh and downsized. For three years now, he had enjoyed a cozy cottage on the beautiful Fraserburgh beach. His office was located downstairs by the living room and kitchen, and his bedroom was upstairs in the loft.

Blake spent many evenings on the balcony looking up at the breathtaking night sky. His life had been a frenetic one. His profession as a buyer had given him many opportunities to network with gallery owners and artists around the world. He could spot talent before others even recognized it, an instinct that had made him both successful and wealthy. He, too, was an artist, though he rarely let himself indulge in his own work anymore. The profits from his career had been handsome, and his investments had given him financial independence. But now, he gloried in the quiet moments. Perhaps too much so. He was never really lonely; nevertheless, a quiet longing always stayed with him—a need for something deeper. A bond that could touch his soul and bring him the peace he didn't know he was searching for.

After unpacking from his trip and having a leisurely stroll on the beach, Blake made a pot of decaf coffee. Then he picked up his phone and called his good friend and mentor, Sid.

Sid answered, "I was wondering if I would hear from you this evening."

Blake declared, "I have arrived and am not too weary for a chat this evening. Are you up for a cup of decaf and conversation on the balcony?"

"Sure, see you in about fifteen."

Sid had been Blake's friend and confidant for over three decades. Both lived and breathed art until retirement. Sid had lost his wife to cancer several years back, and over time, their friendship deepened beyond business. They understood each other—the art world had been good to them, but it had also taken its toll.

Blake heard the front door open and called down the stairs, "Come on up. I've already poured your coffee."

Sid shook hands with Blake and had a seat.

"Do I sense something different? Perhaps finally a more light-hearted Blake?"

Blake sheepishly said, "Maybe."

"A woman!" Sid declared.

"Is it that evident?" Blake exhaled, defeated.

"This is indeed a surprise. I'm listening and want to hear every detail!"

"Her name is Ray."

"Nickname or named after a family member?" Sid asked.

"Must be a family name because it is her middle name."

"How did you meet?"

"My dog strayed, and she found him. I checked with the local vet's office. She had left her name and address with a description of Red. I walked past her beach cottage every morning, so I knew where to go. Guess the rest is history."

"Not so fast! There is a lot of history you've not shared."

Blake hesitated, then admitted, "It is not only chemistry between us. She reveals her soul in what she creates. Even her patio and backyard speak volumes of where her heart resides."

"Give me an example?" Sid asked.

"She appreciates nature and enjoys growing things and promoting good health. Her backyard is a work of art. But what I enjoy most about her is how she lives fully in the moment with little thought of the past or future!"

Sid paused for a moment, nodding thoughtfully. The silence grew awkward until he said, "Sounds like she has experienced many heartaches and hardships and chosen to accept who she is deep in her soul and not allow herself to focus on circumstances that were perhaps laced with struggles and pain. I would say she is a mature and wise woman who can love herself. Does that make sense?"

Blake stared into his coffee cup. "Indeed, it does. You are a wise and discerning man, Sid."

Sid leaned back. "When do you plan to discuss your health with her?"

"Don't know. My health is up to God Almighty and not physicians! You know how I feel about that. Sid, please, let's not talk about it anymore."

Sid sighed. "Okay. I am sorry for bringing it up."

Blake exhaled, shaking off the heaviness of the moment. "I do have a question for you, though. I want to share some of my bucket list adventures with Ray. Help me think of some beautiful places to travel. And, of course, I have not yet mentioned this to her, but I feel in my heart she would want to join me."

Sid's face brightened. "Let's see, I can think of several places right now that would be enchanting, romantic, and adventurous. First on my list would be a trip to Spain to ride horses on the beach. Or Scotland, enjoying trail rides where lodging is available in some of the castles. Another suggestion would be a hiking adventure in Chamonix and Courmayeur. Do you think you could manage this type of activity?"

Blake nodded. "Certainly, if I could take my time."

Sid's excitement grew. "What about a private boat tour in the Amalfi Coast? Sunsets in Santorini? Oh! Or a safari in Tanzania—staying in those luxurious lodges where you wake up to elephants roaming outside your window."

Blake smiled. "That does sound extraordinary."

Sid continued, "And then, there's Japan in the spring—cherry blossoms in Kyoto, staying in a traditional ryokan with hot springs. Or, for something completely different, a trip to Patagonia—mountains, glaciers, and pure, untouched beauty."

Blake laughed, "Now, you're just showing off."

Sid grinned. "You asked for ideas. But truly, Blake, these are the kinds of places that make you feel alive. And if you're thinking about sharing them with Ray, then I'd say you already know how you feel about her."

Blake grew quiet. "It's not as though I'm proceeding with caution. I feel so comfortable with her and confident as well. I just don't want to skip over any part of our journey as we bond. Understand?"

Sid softened. "I do, and I agree. Don't rush and miss out on getting to know all the layers of another's emotions and convictions. That would be cheating yourself and Ray as well."

Sid studied his friend. Blake looked younger, more at ease than he had in years. His heart was seemingly at peace and joyful. Sid hoped Blake's newfound love might lead him to something even deeper—a personal relationship with Christ. He was a good and generous man, loved by many, but it was always obvious that something had eluded him.

Perhaps now, with Ray by his side, he could finally find it.

Chapter Four

Ray plunged her feet deep into the sand as she and Journey watched the setting sun paint the horizon in purples, pinks, and rich amber tones. The beauty of the moment tugged at her, loosening the memories she often tried to keep buried. Some wounds, no matter how much time passed, never fully healed.

Her thoughts drifted to Byron, her beautiful and tenderhearted son. His life in Latvia had been a struggle, spent on the unforgiving streets as the child of parents lost to addiction. Latvia, gripped by a drug epidemic since the seventies, had offered him little hope. She often wondered if she had done enough, if she had given him the life he truly deserved.

A decade later, drugs were sold illegally, and crime and drugs became partners. She had begun the adoption process when he was thirteen, and it was finalized when he was fifteen. As soon as they could, they moved from Latvia back to the States, seeking a fresh start in a place where he could have a real chance. They spent most of their time in her small cabin nestled in Paradise Valley, Montana, a place that felt like heaven on earth.

Byron had just finished high school, barely. He was brilliant in ways that didn't fit within the confines of a classroom. He preferred to learn by doing, by experiencing life firsthand. He had a way with animals, especially horses, and people were naturally drawn to him. But Montana had its own temptations. Marijuana and alcohol were easier to access than structure and discipline, and Byron saw no reason to resist.

Ray had always appreciated his honesty. He never hid who he was or what he struggled with. That was what made it all the more heartbreaking—he was loving, open, and full of potential. She knew deep down that if he couldn't break free from the hold of addiction, it would eventually destroy him. But he didn't see the danger. He didn't see a reason to stop.

After graduating, he enrolled in a trade school. Wanting to support his independence, she bought him a Jeep so he could commute fifteen miles each day. And then, one evening, she received the call she had always been bracing for: he had crashed his car and didn't survive.

The most beautiful young man she had ever known was gone.

The news shattered her. For months, she wandered through the fog of grief, barely surviving. Eventually, the walls of the cabin that had once been their sanctuary became suffocating, filled with ghosts of laughter and moments she could never reclaim. She couldn't stay. She wouldn't.

She sold the cabin—everything in it. She didn't want a single memory to follow her. Then, almost as if fate intervened, *National Geographic* contacted her. They had been interested in her work for years, and after submitting her most prized photographs of Montana, they made her an offer. She became a traveling photographer, paid handsomely for her images, and was given an assignment in Austria as winter approached. She packed her equipment, her ski clothes, and whatever was left of her fractured heart, embracing a solitary life where grief would always be her silent companion.

"Journey, let's return home and grill a steak. I'll prepare a fresh salad from the garden as well. You are learning to love your veggies, aren't you?"

Journey lovingly looked up at her with his deep, intelligent eyes and licked his mouth with his long, red tongue. He had quickly become her closest companion, an unwavering presence in her life.

"I'll race you home!"

With that, the two of them took off along the water's edge, their laughter and barks carried away by the ocean breeze. Ray felt younger than her years in moments like this—light, free, *alive*.

She still loved life, and she loved who she had become: a forty-seven-year-old, healthy, strong woman who felt very much alive. She had a thankful heart that God had comforted, upheld, and shown her how to live well through all of the losses in her life, even with the hollowness of heart she felt.

As they neared the cottage, her steps slowed. From a distance, she spotted Blake sitting in the chair on the front porch with a wide smile. Her heart skipped a beat, maybe several. He stood up, and Journey reached him first, leaping up with excitement. He jumped up and placed his paws on Blake's chest. Blake laughed, rubbing the dog's ears before turning his attention to Ray. As she approached, he stepped forward and wrapped her in an embrace, strong and sure. She felt everything was right at that moment. There was no hesitation, no awkwardness. Just warmth, just home.

"It is good to have you home!" she said, her voice filled with relief and warmth.

"Sounding more like a wife every minute!" he teased, a playful grin spreading across his face.

She rolled her eyes but smiled. "No. Not your wife, just a soul longing to connect with you," she replied softly, her eyes holding a quiet plea for understanding.

Blake's arms tightened around her, his voice thick with emotion, "I've really missed your spirit!"

Ray pulled back slightly, a trace of frustration in her tone, "It wasn't *my* idea that you leave and go halfway around the world!"

Blake chuckled. "What do you say we have a bite to eat and discuss going on some adventures together?"

A slow smile spread across her lips. "I can be ready first thing in the morning," she said with determination, her gaze steady.

Blake laughed and spun her in the sand as he grinned, "I've missed this—missed you!" Journey ran circles around them, caught up in the joy of their reunion.

Ray tilted her head. "How about this? You select from the garden what you'd like, and I will make iced tea and set the table on the patio. Would you like a grilled steak with our mixed greens?"

"But, of course." He responded, his tone playful yet serious. "We're going to need protein. I have a feeling it will be a long night."

"Can you guess what is blooming now?" she asked with a smile, her eyes twinkling with anticipation.

"The moonflowers?" he guessed, a soft smile curving his lips.

"Yes," she answered, her voice filled with quiet reverence. And I enjoyed them in the moonlight last night. They are magnificent, enchanting, and absolutely magical!"

Blake raised an eyebrow. "How can a flower excite someone so much?" he asked, curiosity lacing his words.

Ray's voice softened. "Because it reminds me of my mother. She loved growing things in rich soil. She loved *me* deeply and completely, brought so much balance to my life, and most of all—she loved to laugh. When the moonflowers bloom, it feels like her spirit is dancing all around me."

Blake nodded, understanding. "You were close."

"She was my best friend." Ray exhaled, then smiled. "Now, let's get this meal prepared. We have some catching up to do."

That night, Ray lay in bed, watching the moon through the perfectly placed window. Usually, she disciplined herself to stay in the moment—to not dwell on the past. But tonight, her mind wandered to another place, another time.

Hunza Valley, Pakistan.

She had lived there for two years while on assignment for *National Geographic*, capturing breathtaking landscapes and the essence of the people. Every time she submitted photos, her editor asked her to stay longer. And she had—because, for the first time in a long time, she felt a sense of belonging.

That was where she met Simon.

Simon had a young son, Aman, just eight years old. His wife had been outspoken in political circles, fighting for women's rights in a part of Pakistan where such defiance was dangerous. One morning, she was simply gone—vanished without a trace. Many suspected the government had taken her. By the time Ray arrived, Simon had already been searching for two years.

Her love for Simon and Aman was honest, transparent, *unconditional*. Aman reminded her of Byron—the same curiosity, the same quiet resilience. And for a brief time, they became a family.

Then, one day, Simon's wife returned.

Ray had left quickly, professionally, offering no goodbyes. There had been no need. She knew in her heart that Simon and Aman had felt the same as she had. Some bonds, even in parting, remained unbreakable.

A tear slipped down her cheek. She wept softly, whispering a prayer into the night. Eventually, sleep claimed her, cradled by the moonlight and the warm breeze that sang over her.

Chapter Five

When Blake arrived early the following day, the air was crisp with the scent of salt and blooming wildflowers. Ray was already on the porch, a mug of tea cradled in her hands as she watched the waves roll onto the shore. She greeted him with a warm smile, and together, they settled into a comfortable rhythm of conversation, discussing adventures neither had yet experienced.

Blake brought up horseback riding—Sid's suggestion had stuck with him—but Ray hesitated. "I love horses, but I've had my fill of riding from my days in Montana. Byron and I rode through open fields, under wide skies, for years. It was special, but now... I think I want something different. Something with the sea."

Blake considered this and nodded. "I understand. The ocean has a way of cleansing, of giving us a fresh path forward. What if we went island hopping on a catamaran?"

Ray's face lit up. "Now that excites me! Days spent surrounded by water, discovering new islands, sunsets on the deck, and nothing but the sound of the waves at night... It sounds perfect."

Their decision made, Ray leaned back against her chair, letting the idea settle over her.

"Blake, I'll leave the details of our trip to you, but if you want my help, just say the word. I trust you. We're both used to navigating life independently, and I know you'll plan something amazing."

Blake gave her a thoughtful smile. "Fair enough. I'll talk to my travel agency in the next couple of days. If all goes smoothly, we could leave next week. Sound good?"

"Perfect," Ray agreed.

She set down her tea and glanced at Journey, who was lying at her feet, his tail thumping lazily against the wooden planks of the porch.

"What about Journey?" she asked. "I want to make sure he's in good hands while we're away."

Blake rubbed his jaw, clearly having thought about it too. "I was going to ask if you knew someone you trusted. Maybe someone who could stay here and care for him?"

Ray nodded. "I'll reach out to Saxton. He helped me restore this place and knows a lot of the locals. If anyone can recommend the right person, it's him."

Blake leaned forward. "How long should we arrange for them to stay?"

Ray thought for a moment before deciding. "Three weeks. I know myself—I'll start missing my garden if we're gone much longer than that."

Blake laughed. "Three weeks it is, then."

A quiet pause stretched between them, but it wasn't uncomfortable. It was a moment of understanding, of something deeper stirring beneath the surface.

Ray exhaled softly, then looked at Blake with an intensity that made his breath catch.

"Blake, we barely know each other, and yet, I feel like I've known you forever. It's not just familiarity—it's something deeper. My feelings seem... ancient, as if they've existed beyond time. You have been in my dreams, and those dreams have carried me through the day, awakening parts of me I thought were long asleep. I don't know if this makes sense to you, but—"

Blake reached for her hand, stilling her words. "Ray, I may not have the words the way you do, but I *do* understand. And I feel it too."

She took a shaky breath, her voice softer now. "I believe God has brought us together for a reason—not just for companionship, but to teach us more about ourselves and about Him. I desire His touch in my life, but I also desire the touch of someone who knows Him, who loves Him."

Blake's fingers tightened around hers. "Then let's go forward together. Let's open our hearts to whatever He has planned for us. Let's live in the moment and trust that He is guiding us."

A tear slipped down Ray's cheek as she stepped forward, slipping her arms around him. He held her, steady and strong, as the morning sun cast golden light over the closing moonflower pods—their delicate petals retreating after their midnight bloom, waiting for another night to reveal their beauty once more.

Chapter Six

Tortola quickly became Ray's favorite island. Though she had visited the U.S. Virgin Islands several times, this was her first time in the British Virgin Islands, and it was even more stunning than she had imagined. She and Blake spent their days exploring the sea caves and snorkeling in Smuggler's Cove, where the water stretched in crystal-clear beauty as far as the eye could see.

The catamaran crew met all their expectations. She and Blake both had a master suite of their own, and the husband-and-wife cooking duo, Chase and Lizzie, made each meal an experience to remember. Whenever they anchored close to an island Chase and Lizzie would hike ashore, returning with backpacks full of fresh fruits, vegetables, and seafood. Their energy was infectious, their culinary skills unmatched. They created the most delicious meals and were always upbeat and entertaining.

The captain, Neil, was a seasoned sailor with a wise, easygoing demeanor. He had a way of making even the most unpredictable moments feel like part of the adventure.

At night, the islands twinkled under the moonlight, and Ray found herself mesmerized by their beauty. As she reflected on some of her favorite moments, it was impossible to say what she enjoyed most. The sunsets were unbelievably incredible, and the view from the boat of the islands at night was magical. Sleeping down below with water surrounding them took some getting used to. There were always noticeably gentle rocking and soft sounds of little bubbles gurgling. It took some time to get accustomed to the intermittent squeaks of creaking wood. Neil had given the perfect explanation for the singing wood. The boat was designed to bend and not break, so the engineering and molding were flexible in the wood. That thought comforted her—until the night it didn't.

Even though their extravagant adventure had been breathtakingly beautiful in limitless measure, Ray was homesick.

As she drifted off to sleep, she heard the boat groaning, and then she tumbled to the floor. Above, she heard Neil hollering, "Stay below!" She crawled to Blake's suite. It took all the strength and will she had to navigate with the boat leaning to the side. She knew a terrible storm must have swept in upon them because the ship twisted and groaned… if she could only get to Blake. There were many things she had never shared with him. Both had enjoyed one another's company immensely, but some of her heartfelt feelings had not been expressed.

She heard him calling her name, "Ray, are you okay?"

She called to him, "Yes. I'm at your doorway; can you open the door?"

"I'm trying; it's jammed!"

"I'm going to push with my legs, and you pull!"

Finally, both pried the door open enough for Blake to squeeze out. Ray grabbed him, and both toppled over against the hallway wall, clinging to each other.

Her tears spilled onto his chest as she whispered, "I was so scared."

Blake cupped her face, his voice firm yet filled with warmth. "Ray, we're going to be okay. I promise. We still have some living to do, and I want to live the rest of my life with you. I love you, my darling. I have loved you from the time I laid eyes on you."

A sob escaped her lips, but this time, it wasn't from fear. "Oh, Blake, I love you, too, and I want to spend the rest of my life with you."

There was another jolt of the boat, and both slid together down the little hallway. They heard Neil holler, "Man overboard!"

Blake's eyes darkened with urgency. "Ray, stay here. I will try to climb the steps and see if I can help."

She wanted to protest, to beg him to stay, but her throat tightened with fear. All she could do was nod, gripping the doorframe as he climbed toward the chaos.

The storm was fierce. She cried out to God to help them all, but most of all, to calm the storm. And He did. Within a few minutes, the boat was still and then gradually resumed its normal, upright position.

Moments later, Blake reappeared, soaked to the bone but safe. Without hesitation, he pulled her into his arms.

"I believe things are manageable on deck now. Carson, one of the crew members, was thrown overboard during the storm, and after casting a couple of throw bags, Neil could finally bring him onboard. He may have some injuries, but nothing life-threatening. The squall took us off course so we will land at Anegada, and from there, I'll secure our transportation home."

Ray let out a shaky breath, pressing her forehead against his chest. "Blake, I'll be so glad to get home."

He kissed the top of her head, holding her close. "So will I, Ray. So will I."

Chapter Seven

Ray sat contentedly on her patio, cradling a glass of sweet tea in her hands as she watched the moonflowers sway under the silver glow of the night. She relished these moments with the symphony of night creatures surrounding her. Beside her, Journey slept soundly, his paws twitching as if he were chasing something in his dreams. Every now and then, he whimpered softly, only to settle back into deep, rhythmic breaths.

She sighed, feeling the weight of Blake's absence. He had left the day before, and though it had only been a short time, she already missed his presence—the steady warmth of his companionship, the strength of his embrace, the way he listened to her with such depth.

They had returned to Cayman the previous week, slipping seamlessly back into their routines. Ray had no desire for another grand adventure. Neither, she suspected, did Blake. They had talked about marriage, about what it would mean to merge their lives after years of independence. But there were still things to work through—his daughter, Rachel, being one of them.

Blake had taken a quick flight to Miami on Cayman Airways and planned to rent a car and meet his daughter in Naples. He also wanted to browse the Naples Art Gallery on 5th Avenue and meet a new artist whose work he thought was exceptional. This young man had little exposure to areas that would promote profits for him. He believed in the artist's potential and wanted to introduce him to a broader audience, possibly even European galleries. It was one of the many things she admired about Blake—his ability to see beyond what was and imagine what could be.

Ray looked down at Journey and whispered, "Come on, boy, let's go to bed. The sandman has already visited us tonight."

Yet as she lay in bed, sleep evaded her. Her thoughts flitted from one thing to another—a rare occurrence for someone who usually embraced the present moment with ease. She understood now how people could create their own anxiety. It wasn't the circumstances that weighed them down, but their inability to let go of the past or their fear of the future.

More than anything, she longed to keep her heart pure before God. She knew that with a pure heart, one could see beyond the surface—into the hidden depths of the Creator's wisdom.

Softly, she prayed, *"Dear God, I'm not certain that Blake fully relies on Your Holy Spirit. I know he believes in You, but I ask that You draw him into a deeper relationship with Your Son, Jesus. Let him experience Your presence in a way that transforms him. Lord, when I think of marriage, I long to be equally yoked. You have led me since I was a child, teaching me how to love with Your love while also guarding my heart with discernment. I ask You now, precious Lord, to guide me in Your perfect will. Amen."*

A sudden gust of wind rushed through the open window, knocking over her bedside lamp. Startled, she sat up and made a mental note to check the weather in the morning.

The next day, Ray woke early, determined to find Pastor Lovell at Cayman Islands Baptist Church. She had attended services there occasionally since moving to Cayman, always drawn to the simplicity of his message: **Place your faith in Jesus Christ and always have a thankful heart.** Today, she hoped he could provide wise counsel about her future with Blake. More than that, she wanted him to officiate their wedding. She desired a covenant marriage—one that could withstand the inevitable storms of life.

"Come on, Journey," she called, scratching behind his ears. "How about some fresh blueberries with your kibble?"

She stepped outside to gather berries and greens, but another strong gust of wind knocked the container from her hands, sending fruit rolling across the patio. A strange unease settled in her chest. She went inside and turned on her phone to check the weather.

A tropical storm was moving in from the southwest.

Cayman had been spared many times before, which was one of the reasons she had always felt safe here. Still, she didn't want to take any chances. She ate a quick bowl of oatmeal, fed Journey, and then set about securing her cottage. She locked down the outside shutters—her usual precaution before any turbulent weather.

Then, she grabbed her keys and called for Journey to hop into the car. It had been a while since she had driven, as most of her favorite places were within walking distance. But today, she needed to get to the church.

Her Mini Cooper Countryman still looked as good as new, despite its years. Journey sat tall in the passenger seat, his tongue hanging out in excitement, as if sensing an adventure ahead.

Ray glanced at him and smiled. "Alright, boy, we're off to church to find Pastor Lovell. And if this storm gets any stronger, we'll make ourselves comfortable there until it passes."

As she pulled onto the road, a deep peace settled over her. She didn't know what the coming days would bring. But she knew one thing for certain—she would trust in the One who did.

Chapter Eight

Blake's flight to Miami had been smooth, and his rental car was ready the moment he landed. He appreciated the efficiency—it allowed him to hit the road and reach Naples before dark. Rachel had chosen the restaurant for their dinner and even made a special request for him to wear a coat and tie. That alone was enough to tell him it would be a formal evening.

As he stepped inside King Pins, he spotted Rachel immediately. She stood beside the hostess, gesturing toward a private table, her poised demeanor reminding him so much of her mother. His heart swelled with affection. No matter how much time passed, she would always be his little girl.

"Hello, Dad. How was your flight?"

"Perfect."

"Just wondering, because there's a storm brewing below Cuba."

Blake's stomach tightened. A storm? He had been so focused on this trip that he hadn't checked the weather in Cayman before leaving.

"When did you last check for an update?" he asked, his voice sharper than intended.

Rachel shrugged. "Dad, relax. You're here, safe. No need to worry about an impending storm. It's likely to shift east and fizzle out before hitting land."

The hostess led them to their table, tucked into a private corner adorned with red roses. The ambiance was ideal—soft lighting, hushed conversations, and music at just the right volume to allow for an intimate talk.

Blake exhaled, trying to shake the unease settling in his gut. But his thoughts kept drifting back to Ray.

Rachel studied him. "Dad, you look anxious. Is everything okay?"

"Yes, I'm fine," he said, brushing off her concern. "Let's talk about the menu. What looks good?"

"I'm getting the lobster bisque and the broiled sea bass," she said. "And you?"

"My appetite isn't strong tonight. I'll just have mixed greens with grilled salmon."

Rachel raised an eyebrow. "Fish and veggies? That doesn't sound like you. Eating healthy these days?"

"You could say that," he said, allowing a small smile. "I have a friend in Cayman who has a garden. Fresh vegetables are a part of my diet now."

She tilted her head, curiosity evident. "A friend? Or someone… special?"

Blake met her gaze. "Someone very special. We're planning to get married."

Rachel's expression froze. Then, she leaned back in her chair. "I hope she's not after your money."

Blake sighed. "Rachel, give me some credit. Do you really think I'd stay single all these years only to fall for someone who doesn't love me for who I am?"

She huffed. "Dad, women can be sneaky."

"She isn't," he assured her. "Ray is independent, secure, and comfortable in her own life."

Rachel crossed her arms. "Is she financially stable?"

He nodded. "Yes. More than capable of standing on her own two feet."

Rachel shook her head. "Still, Dad, you don't have to rush into marriage. You can be with her without making it official."

Blake frowned. "Is that the kind of advice you'd want me to give you?"

"I guess," she muttered.

"I hope your values aren't becoming... worldly, Rachel. Marriage is a sacred covenant, something God ordains. I would hope you believe in doing what's right."

Rachel rolled her eyes. "Dad, you sound like you're stuck in the last century."

"No," he said firmly. "I just believe in living with integrity. I thought you did, too."

She sighed. "Let's not argue. I don't want to talk about your girlfriend, values, or whatever else. I actually wanted to discuss a business opportunity—one I want you to partner with me on."

Blake took a slow breath, forcing himself to shift gears. "Alright, I'm listening."

Rachel laid out her investment idea over dinner, her excitement evident. Blake promised to look into it and give it serious thought. By the time they parted ways, he was relieved the conversation had ended on a lighter note.

But as soon as he checked into his hotel, his mind snapped back to Ray.

He tried calling her—once, twice, three times. No answer.

He called again in the middle of the night. Still nothing.

A pit formed in his stomach. Something wasn't right. Not even during the catamaran squall had he felt this helpless.

Chapter Nine

Ray and Journey remained at the church along with many others overnight until the last trails of the storm had passed. Cayman had weathered many storms and hurricanes. For the last decade or so, most storms took paths around the islands, and the locals said that God had shown much favor to the people of the Cayman Islands. Ray certainly felt that Almighty God was in total control.

Driving back to her cottage took longer than usual because sand covered the roads. The winds had not seemed strong, but the sand had been redistributed. The breeze was pleasant now. Journey's expression looked as though he were smiling at everyone with his head extended out of the passenger window. She had fallen in love with him.

She arrived home safely, drove the car into the garage, and whistled for Journey. As she stepped onto the sand-covered driveway, her feet sunk at least three inches. She loved the texture of Cayman's sand. It was almost as fine as flour. She loved to dig her feet deep into it, just like a child. She was thankful that her losses had not diminished the child in her. Lately, she felt more like a child than ever before. She was full of faith and hope. Her Creator seemed real, personal, and ever-present.

After unlocking the cottage's outside shutters, she walked immediately to her garden area. Everything looked untouched: no damage, no sand. Even her moonflower blooms were still intact. *Heavenly Father, how gracious you are to me. Thank you.*

Ray realized that her cell phone service had not been restored and knew that if Blake had tried to reach her, he would be concerned at this point. These things would all work out in God's timing, and she would remain peaceful.

She gathered fresh blueberries, prepared coffee, and baked blueberry scones. Journey enjoyed his usual kibble with a few blueberries. She took her morning coffee and sat in one of the chairs out front. The ocean was still troubled somewhat, but the morning sky was a reassuring brilliant blue. She dug her bare feet into the soft sand and beckoned Journey to sit beside her. She reveled in the moment.

After coffee and scones for breakfast, Ray and Journey went for a romp on the beach. She walked several miles, picking up beautiful shells and coral the storm had washed ashore. She thought about the discussion she and Pastor Lovell had about marriage. A covenant marriage was much more than loving someone and deciding to get married. It was a commitment to your spouse and God—an eternal commitment. She hoped Blake understood the seriousness of such a union; otherwise, she could not marry him.

Suddenly, she felt her cell phone vibrate in her pocket. She had a voicemail message from Blake. As she surmised, he was concerned that he could not reach her.

She called his number, and he answered immediately. "I've been so worried about you, Ray. Is everything okay?"

"Yes, I just now have my cell service restored. Journey and I are doing fine. We stayed the night at our church. My cottage and your villa are okay. There was no storm damage. I would say the only evidence from the storm is misplaced sand. It covered the roads back to my place."

"I'm so relieved to hear your voice and that all is well."

"How is your visit going with Rachel?"

"Honestly, Ray, I could not enjoy my visit with Rachel last night because of the storm. All I could think of was making sure you were okay."

"Blake, we must place our trust in the Lord. After all, He is in control."

"Just maybe I miss you. Let's not have any more parting after this, okay?"

"Great plan. Now, what are your plans for the day?"

"I plan to visit my favorite gallery here and inquire about the young artist I've been interested in. I can assure you that after talking with you, I'll have a grand day with peace of mind."

"Blake, I wish for you a day sprinkled with serendipity! Catch that vision."

"I shall. I promise. Now you and Journey have fun. I'll call you tonight and let you know about my return flight. I love you."

"We love you, too. Bye."

Ray slipped her phone back into her pocket, a warm smile lingering on her lips. Blake loves me. The thought was as comforting as the gentle sea breeze brushing against her skin. Journey sat beside her, his head tilted as if sensing her relief.

"Well, boy," she said, ruffling his ears, "looks like we'll be seeing Blake soon."

Journey wagged his tail, his golden fur catching the morning light. The storm had passed, leaving behind a sense of renewal—not just in the island's landscape but in Ray's heart as well.

She took another sip of coffee, letting the warmth settle inside her. The ocean was still restless, the waves rolling in with a bit more force than usual, but the sky was an unshaken blue. Peace after the storm.

Her thoughts drifted back to Pastor Lovell's words. A covenant marriage wasn't just about love; it was about commitment, faith, and trusting God's plan. She knew she loved Blake, but did he fully understand what marriage meant to her? Would he be ready to make that kind of promise before God?

She glanced at Journey, who had started digging in the sand, completely lost in the moment. *That's how I want to live—grounded in faith, present in each moment, and trusting that God has already mapped out the path ahead.*

She closed her eyes and whispered, "Lord, let Your will be done."

Chapter Ten

Blake was excited about his mission of finding the young artist Rihards Giddings. As he entered his favorite gallery, his expectancy of success filled him with excitement, hope and confirmation of a marvelous adventure.

"Well, Mr. Forsyth, it has been quite a while since you've graced our gallery with your presence. Very good to see you."

Blake shook hands with the man. "Randall, I was not sure I would find you still dabbling in art here in Naples. It is good to see you again."

"Thought you were retired, but once an artist, always an artist, right?"

"I am retired and still living in Scotland, but I'm staying in Cayman this summer. I have recently read about a young artist who interests me, and I want to meet him and see more of his work. This is not something to do with business; it is just a keen interest of mine. I cannot tell you why. It is just a strong feeling in my spirit that this young man could benefit from someone taking an interest in him and, perhaps, promoting his work. I have no desire to partner with anyone at this point in my life, only to encourage another in life's adventures. Does that make sense?"

"Yes. Similar to paying it forward."

"That's a great way to look at this present interest of mine. Does the name Rihards Giddings ring a bell?"

"Yes, it does. I like his work and believe that, given the chance, he could succeed. His work has much promise. Would you like to see some of his paintings?"

"Of course. That's what I was hoping for!"

"Follow me to the back of the gallery. I am storing a few of his oils for him until he returns to the States. Someone in his family died last week, so he flew home and asked me to store a few canvases until he returned. He sold at least a dozen paintings at an exhibit here a few weeks back. His work is magnetic, but complex in that one initially is taken by a delightful scene, and yet when the canvas is studied, there are things that surface and stir your spirit with questions about the artist himself."

"That is exactly why I want to meet this young man and see more of his art. All of us are searching for hidden secrets, are we not?"

"Blake, I could not express the true meaning of art any better. Most people who purchase art pieces don't understand that they are buying a piece of the artist's heart. Here we are. I have left his paintings on easels in the event someone comes in asking to see his work. Very promising, don't you think?"

As Blake surveyed the art pieces, only one thought came to mind: this young man was destined for success!

"Randall, I would like to take a few photos of his art, if you don't mind."

"Help yourself. What are your plans, Blake?"

"First, I want to purchase all these paintings: name your price. Then, I want you to secure them for shipping carefully. I would like you to ship to an address in Cayman. Next, I would ask that you give Rihards my name and number and tell him I'm interested in exhibiting his work in Cayman as soon as he can produce at least four more paintings before we have a showing for him. And, of course, I would request his presence at the exhibit. I will make travel arrangements and send him a check to cover his expenses."

"Blake, I'm confident this young man will be encouraged and grateful to accept your terms. His life has not been an easy one. Even though he always seems positive, he is presently struggling to survive. The sale of his paintings did not provide him with much profit. I even wondered how he would manage the expense of flying back to the States after his stay in Latvia. I would say you are a Godsend."

After leaving the art gallery, Blake called Rachel. "Good morning. How would you like to have lunch with me in the gallery district at an outdoor table?"

"Yes. I could do that, Dad. What time and where?"

"You tell me. I do not have a schedule."

"Okay. See you at Harper's Cafe at noon, and we'll eat outside in a shady spot under the umbrellas."

Blake was excited about his visit with Rachel since his head was now clear. He could hardly remember any of their conversation from the night before.

Blake walked to the café with a renewed sense of purpose coursing through him. This is what life is about—recognizing talent, offering a hand where it's needed, and trusting that God places certain people in our paths for a reason. He had no doubt that Rihards Giddings was destined for something greater, and he was eager to be a part of the young artist's journey.

His phone buzzed in his pocket. Rachel. He had invited her to lunch, hoping for a lighter, more meaningful conversation than their strained dinner the night before.

"Hey, Dad," Rachel called out, already seated under a large umbrella at Harper's Café. She looked poised as always, but there was a guardedness in her eyes that Blake wished he could ease.

Blake leaned in and gave her a warm hug before sitting down. "You're looking lovely today, Rachel."

She smiled but cut straight to the point. "I must say, Dad, you look much better than last night. Did you finally get some sleep?"

"Not sure about that, but I feel invigorated," Blake admitted. "Like I've stepped into a new season of my life."

Rachel raised an eyebrow. "A new season? Sounds poetic."

"More like purposeful." He reached for a menu, but his mind was still on Rihards' paintings, the layered brushstrokes, the silent messages hidden within the colors. "I found an artist today, Rachel. A young man who reminds me why I fell in love with art in the first place."

"I thought you retired from all that," she said, sipping her iced tea.

"I did. But this is different. I don't want to profit from his work—I want to help him succeed. To pay it forward."

Rachel's expression was unreadable. "Huh. I've never seen this side of you before."

Blake smiled. "Neither have I. But it feels right."

Rachel sighed and leaned back in her chair. "I just hope your new girlfriend isn't filling your head with dreams of vapor."

Blake's jaw tightened, but instead of responding with frustration, he reached for her hand. "Rachel, that was unkind. I wish you would meet Ray before making assumptions. She's a remarkable woman—independent, talented, and filled with wisdom."

Rachel looked away, clearly uncomfortable. Blake could see that the idea of him moving on after all these years unsettled her. Perhaps she feared change, or maybe she just didn't want to share him with someone else.

"Fine," she muttered, picking up the menu. "Let's order quickly. I have somewhere to be."

Blake sighed inwardly but didn't push the matter. Instead, he chose patience.

As they waited for their meals, he decided to speak from the heart. "Rachel, I know your mother and I made choices that affected you. I regret that we weren't always the best example. But if I can offer you one piece of advice, it's this: stand on a platform of integrity. In business. In life. Let God guide your decisions."

Rachel rolled her eyes. "Let's leave praying to the nuns, okay? They had plenty of authority back in the school you and Mom sent me to."

Blake exhaled slowly, feeling the weight of years of distance between them. "I just want what's best for you, Rachel. That's all."

Rachel's expression softened, but she quickly masked it. "Then do your research on my business investment, Dad. Help me accumulate wealth the way you did. Fair enough?"

Blake studied her, wishing she wanted more than just financial success. Wishing she understood that wealth wasn't the measure of a full life.

"Promise me you'll visit me in Cayman soon?" he asked.

Rachel smirked. "Promise me you'll partner with me on this investment."

Blake chuckled. "I promise to do my research and get back to you."

Rachel nodded. "Then we have a deal."

As they ate, Blake couldn't help but feel that they were speaking different languages—his heart set on purpose, hers set on profit.

Still, God wasn't finished writing their story.

And neither was he.

Chapter Eleven

The sky that morning stretched over miles and miles in an explosion of black, pink, and mahogany red, the most breathtaking dawn Ray had ever seen. It was as if the morning itself was singing a new song of hope into her spirit.

She spotted Blake in the distance, and before she could take another step, he was running toward her.

They met in a tight embrace, holding onto each other as if they had been apart for years instead of days.

"It is wonderful to be home," Blake murmured between kisses.

Ray's heart swelled. "I'm glad you feel this is your home now."

Blake cupped her face, his voice tender. "Sweetheart, you are home to me. Surely, you must know that by now. Wherever we live, as long as you're by my side, I will be at home."

She smiled up at him, her heart full. "Come. Let's walk to the cottage so I can prepare breakfast. I want to hear all about your trip—your visit with Rachel and the artist you spoke so favorably about!"

They joined hands, strolling along the shore, while Journey ran joyful circles around them, his tail wagging wildly.

Back at the cottage, Ray set to work making breakfast. The aroma of fresh coffee filled the air as she prepared a platter of fresh fruit to accompany the blueberry scones she had baked the night before.

She called out to Blake, who was relaxing on the patio. "Do you want fresh-squeezed orange juice or grape juice?"

"Grape juice, please."

Ray grinned. "Hey, I could air fry some bacon for us, too. We'll need protein for today's agenda."

Blake chuckled. "That sounds great."

Once breakfast was finished, they lingered over a second cup of coffee, soaking in the stillness of the morning. The world felt untouched, as if it belonged only to them.

Blake exhaled contentedly. "Ray, this place is a little paradise. Every time I sit here, breathing in the fresh, fragrant air, I feel at peace. And your koi—they're growing so fast. They add such a calming presence to your backyard."

Ray smiled. "I need living things around me. Journey is such a bonus—he fills my cup every day. Animals are some of God's most delightful creations, don't you think?"

Blake nodded. "Journey has grown dear to me since meeting you. And you—you see things differently. It's like you see with your spirit rather than just your eyes." He paused, his voice full of emotion. "You've added a new dimension to my life, Ray. You've given me hope."

Ray reached for his hand. "Blake, maybe this is a season in your life where God is bestowing eternal hope. That's our real hope in this earthly passage."

Blake considered her words. "Perhaps you're right."

Ray leaned in, eager to hear about his latest adventure. "Tell me about this artist you discovered in Naples. You were really excited about him."

Blake's eyes lit up. "I want to bring him here and sponsor an art exhibit. Do you know of any place nearby where I could set up a small gallery?"

Ray thought for a moment. "Honestly, no, but I'll give Saxton a call. He always knows what's available."

Blake grinned. "Brilliant idea."

Ray hesitated before asking her next question. "And how was your visit with Rachel? I'm sure you two had a lot to talk about."

Blake sighed. "Not really. The main thing she shared was that she wants me to invest in a business venture. I told her I would research it, which I did last night."

Ray tilted her head. "And what do you think? Good investment or risky?"

"Definitely risky. I found very few solid facts—mostly speculation. I'm going to decline and suggest she do the same."

Ray gave him a reassuring look. "Perhaps once you share the facts, or lack of facts, from your research, she'll be grateful you saved her from a financial disaster."

Blake exhaled. "I hope you're right, but something tells me she won't take the news well. Still, I'll give her a call today and let her know my decision."

Ray squeezed his hand. "And I'll call Saxton so we can find you the perfect gallery space."

Blake hesitated, then turned to face her fully. "Ray... can we talk about our marriage plans now?"

Ray smirked playfully. "I don't recall receiving a proposal on bended knee."

Blake grinned mischievously, then dropped to one knee and pulled a small, dark blue velvet box from his jacket pocket.

"Will you marry me?"

Ray gasped. "Blake, you are full of surprises! You've completely caught me off guard!"

Blake's blue eyes twinkled. "I'm waiting patiently for your answer—on bended knee!"

Tears welled in Ray's eyes. "My answer is YES!"

Blake opened the box, revealing a platinum band adorned with three exquisite diamonds. Inside the band, an inscription read BF ~ RB.

Ray's breath caught. "Oh, Blake, this is the most beautiful ring I've ever seen. The diamonds are breathtaking."

Blake beamed. "I loved shopping for your ring. I approached it the same way I approach discovering great art. I found a jeweler in Canada—he's connected to De Beers, and he designed this especially for you."

Ray traced the delicate band. "De Beers? I've heard of them. What's their motto?"

Blake's voice was soft. "Love and commitment."

Tears spilled down Ray's cheeks. "Oh, Blake… how perfect. The ring reflects the heart of the giver. This ring sings your song, my dear. It's the perfect fit for both of us."

Blake slipped it onto her finger, then pulled her into a deep kiss. The sunrise had brought more than a new day—it had ushered in a new beginning.

Chapter Twelve

August was a whirlwind month. Both Blake and Ray were busy with details for their wedding and the new art gallery. Sid had flown in to help Blake with the gallery details. Both men were in their element, especially since this project was all about helping the young artist Rihards, who would be flying in during the middle of September when the gallery would have its grand opening.

It was decided that the marriage ceremony would be on September 3rd in the evening on the beach. Pastor Lovell had counseled them both and felt they were ready to commit to a covenant marriage. Saxton and a couple of Ray's closest neighbors had inquired about taking charge of a reception after the marriage ceremony. Plus, several individuals at the church wanted to contribute and honor the couple in celebration of their union. Ray and Blake were deeply touched by the outpouring of love and generosity surrounding their union.

Ray and Saxton had worked tirelessly designing the art gallery. There were partitions that needed to come down and be replaced with glass panels. Ray had purchased silk flower arrangements, pedestals, a receptionist's desk, two contemporary lamps, and comfortable chairs to place beside a small glass end table for intimate conversations when customers needed time to ponder their decisions. She had also placed a small refrigerator in the storage area for fresh fruit and sparkling water, should refreshments be offered.

Blake finally persuaded Ray to display a dozen or so photographs on one of the gallery panels during the grand opening. At first, she was hesitant, but after much discussion, she asked Saxton to make frames for the photographs Blake selected.

While the excitement built, Blake faced disappointment in his relationship with Rachel. She had declined his invitation to the wedding, stating she had secured an investor for her business venture—the same one Blake had advised against. Their last conversation had been strained, with Rachel voicing disapproval of both his upcoming marriage and his financial choices.

"You're making a mistake, Dad. Both of your decisions—turning down my business opportunity and marrying someone you barely know—are unwise and costly."

Blake had only responded with quiet patience. "Rachel, I love you. I hope you'll visit soon."

He wished things were different, but he had made peace with his decisions.

Ray had done an extensive search for a wedding band for Blake. She wanted something meaningful that spoke to both of them. She finally discovered the perfect ring. It was handcrafted with a 14-karat gold band, four aquamarine accents, and a mother-of-pearl inlay. She requested a delivery date of a week prior to the wedding, and true to the jeweler's word, it had been designed and delivered in a timely fashion.

Ray's neighbor, Aria, had volunteered to make Ray's wedding dress. Ray never dreamed that creating a simple dress could be such a journey and a time of bonding for two women. Aria was gifted and had many creative suggestions regarding the wedding dress. Aria was in her late twenties and single. She had been born on the island and had family close by. She had established a business as a seamstress and furnished some of the boutiques with unique beach dresses and scarves.

Ray and Aria enjoyed selecting material online. There were many options, but finally, a decision was made to purchase five yards of ivory double silk satin in the color 'eminence'. The material was exquisite, and the lace veil with tiny pearls completed Ray's evening attire.

Aria had strung and arranged tiny solar lights around the koi pool in Ray's backyard area. She wanted to create a romantic and enchanting atmosphere for their honeymoon night. She had also ordered silk sheets and a lightweight summer quilt made of bamboo for Ray's bedroom. In addition, she planned to arrange candles in strategic places throughout the cottage and light them before the couple returned after the reception.

Sid had ordered Blake's wedding attire from a gentleman's shop in London. The trousers were a light bluish-gray color and made of silk. The loose-fitting, lightweight silk shirt was the same color as Ray's gown. A muted blue satin vest and a solid navy silk tie completed the outfit. Since Blake was focused on many of the details concerning the gallery, he was thankful for Sid's help with his wedding attire and was confident it would complement Ray's wedding gown. Sid was never opinionated, and his mild manner behind the scenes seamlessly placed icing on the cake for every project and event he was involved in. One would think he had been trained and groomed for royalty.

With so much behind them and even more ahead, Blake and Ray carved out a week for themselves—a time to pause, reflect, and simply be.

Their new chapter was about to begin, and they wanted to step into it not exhausted, but refreshed—ready to embrace love, art, and the beautiful unknown of forever.

Chapter Thirteen

Sid and Blake sat on the villa balcony and relaxed in the comfortable silence as they beheld a magnificent sunset over the ocean. The sky was a symphony of gold, deep purple, and sapphire blue, casting a sacred stillness over the moment.

For both men, these quiet evenings were a sanctuary—a place where they could reflect, not just on the beauty of creation, but on the Creator Himself. Some thoughts were meant to be spoken; others were meant to be pondered in the solitude of the soul.

After a long pause, Sid's voice broke the silence, gentle yet firm.

"What about your health, Blake?"

Blake remained still.

"I know you must feel convicted to tell Ray before the wedding."

Another pause—longer this time, heavier.

Sid leaned forward slightly. "You do want to tell her the truth before making this lifelong commitment, don't you?"

Blake exhaled, running a hand through his hair. "The more time passes, the harder it gets." His voice was low, almost strained. "Because then I have to explain why I haven't told her sooner."

He stared out at the darkening sky. "I've been lost in every moment with her, Sid. For the first time in years, I feel alive. And every time I think about the future, I push the truth away."

Sid nodded. He understood. But understanding didn't change what needed to be done.

"Blake, all my life, I've heard Christians say, 'The truth will set you free.'" Sid's voice was steady, his words intentional. "That's scripture. That's Jesus."

Blake let the words settle before he whispered, "I don't have the kind of faith you and Ray have."

Sid shook his head. "Faith isn't about human effort. It's about what Jesus gives us—what He writes on our hearts. It's supernatural."

Blake let out a bitter chuckle. "Maybe there's a part of me that just can't let go. Can't fully surrender to God's will."

Sid smiled softly. "You just said it."

Blake closed his eyes. The weight of truth pressed against him—heavy, unavoidable. "Tomorrow. I'll tell Ray tomorrow."

He swallowed hard. "But Sid, I'm terrified. What if she changes her mind? What if I lose her?"

Sid reached for Blake's hand, gripping it firmly. "Let me pray for you."

Blake's voice was barely above a whisper. "Please."

Sid bowed his head.

"Holy Father in Heaven, we are but clay. You are the potter, the Creator of our souls, the Designer of our lives, and the Orchestrator of every moment on this earthly journey. Tonight, we lay our fears, our wills, and our burdens at the foot of the cross. Father, Your will alone will be done. Place Your faith within my dear friend, Blake. He is knocking at Your door, searching for the path You would have him walk. Let him find peace in surrender. In Jesus' Name, let it be. Amen."

When Sid lifted his head, tears streaked Blake's face.

Neither spoke. The only sound was the ocean's rhythmic breathing and the rustling wind that suddenly picked up in intensity.

A gust swept across the balcony, knocking over the table between them. The coffee cups shattered against the concrete, their pieces scattering across the floor.

Blake stared at the broken fragments, his voice raw. "I feel like those cups right now."

Sid placed a hand on his shoulder. "Our Lord heals the broken-hearted."

Blake swallowed hard. "Maybe that's where real freedom is found."

Sid gave a knowing nod, his voice gentle but sure. "Yes, within total surrender."

Chapter Fourteen

Blake set out on his morning walk to Ray's cottage. There was a strong breeze that felt cleansing to his soul, and he increased his pace with abandonment of being preoccupied by his thoughts or intentions. He felt free and unencumbered since Sid's prayer for him; he reveled in total peace. His soul and his mind seemed suspended in a peace he had never witnessed in his life. His only desire was to give his life to God and live his life for God, the one True God who had saved him. For a moment, he thought about what being saved really meant. Having eternal life came to mind first, and then knowing and experiencing divine love from Jesus and being saved from one's own desires and control.

Journey ran to greet him before he reached the gate. "Hey, boy. How are you doing? Where is your owner?"

Ray opened the door and waved. "I'm so glad you came early. I just finished preparing breakfast; come join me on the patio!"

Blake grabbed her and pulled her close. She tilted her head toward his face, tenderly kissed his lips, and held him longer than usual.

Blake took a deep breath. "Ray, I need to have a serious talk with you this morning."

A flicker of understanding passed through her eyes. "I don't know what it is, but I sensed in my spirit that you had something important to tell me."

She reached for his hand. "Come on in. Let's eat and talk on the patio."

As they walked together, she asked, "Is it okay if we finish breakfast first before we dive into what's on your mind?"

Blake nodded. "Of course."

They sat together at the small patio table, Journey resting at their feet, his soft brown eyes shifting between them. The koi swam joyfully in the pool nearby, more active than usual. Blake loved everything about Ray's home—it was a reflection of her spirit, her love for beauty, and her devotion to God's creation.

When the meal was finished, he didn't wait any longer.

"Ray, I owe you an apology for not telling you this sooner. There's no excuse, other than the fact that I was a coward." His voice was steady, but his hands trembled slightly as he reached for hers. "I was diagnosed with lung cancer two years ago."

Ray froze. Her breath caught in her throat, and before she could stop them, tears sprang to her eyes.

Blake noticed immediately. He pulled his chair closer to hers, holding both of her hands tightly in his.

"I have three tumors in my left lung. So far, I feel no effects, and besides my doctors, only you and Sid know about my condition."

Ray swallowed hard, gripping his hands even tighter.

"We'll go through this journey together, Blake." Her voice was steady, filled with conviction and love.

Blake studied her face, searching for any trace of fear or hesitation. He found none.

She continued, "I can understand why you didn't want to tell me. I think we both have things we keep locked away—not because we want to hide them, but because we don't want them to overshadow the joy of the present."

Blake exhaled, relief washing over him. "Ray, I couldn't have said it better myself. Still, sweetheart, I'm sorry I waited so long."

She shook her head. "We both have pasts, Blake. We both have things that will surface in time. That's part of life, part of love. But if we trust Jesus to lead us, then we'll have everything we need to trust each other too."

His throat tightened. "Ray, the grace you give others is rare. Thank you."

She gave him a soft smile and squeezed his hands. "I think we should set this conversation aside for now. Let's take these dishes inside and go for a walk on the beach."

Journey's ears perked up, sensing the excitement in her voice. He leapt up, wagging his tail, ready for the adventure ahead.

Chapter Fifteen

The big day had finally arrived. The sun hovered low in the sky, casting golden hues over the ocean. The air carried the scent of salt and jasmine, and the soft lull of the waves provided nature's own wedding hymn.

Saxton, Aria, and Sid had meticulously arranged every detail—from the flower-woven altar to the elegant table covering that shimmered with delicate beading.

Pastor Lovell and a few congregation members had prepared food for the reception and placed a lovely flower arrangement in the center of the table. Aria had designed and created a unique table covering: white with glistening beads sewn around the edge. The table was set off to the side of the altar where the ceremony would take place. Sid had secured a florist to weave pink roses throughout Saxton's altar on the sand. Aria attached light pink chiffon streamers along the top of the altar. All the details had been perfectly orchestrated.

As the sun began setting, Pastor Lovell invited everyone to sit on the sand where white satin comforters had been placed. He walked to the altar and bowed his head.

And then, they appeared.

Blake and Ray, hand in hand, walked from the cottage, silhouetted by the magnificent backdrop of a pink and yellow sky reflected on the aqua waves. Blake's tie and loose silk sleeves fluttered in the wind, while Ray's gown—soft and radiant—hugged her form as if the wind itself had sculpted it around her. Her veil lifted and twirled above them, as if the heavens were blessing their union.

They slowed as they neared the altar, pausing to take in the vast, endless horizon. Aria, knowing this moment was priceless, raised her camera. This picture, she knew, belonged somewhere special.

The ceremony was intimate, reverent—a covenant marriage before God. Blake's voice trembled only slightly as he vowed his love, and when Pastor Lovell finally said, "You may kiss your bride," he did so with a tenderness that spoke of deep devotion.

Cheers and applause rose against the sound of the waves, and soon the small group was laughing, embracing, and celebrating. Pastor Lovell's team had prepared a simple yet elegant spread for the reception, with fresh island fruit, delicate pastries, and sparkling cider.

Saxton, ever the artist, brought out his guitar, strumming a soft melody. Blake pulled Ray close, leading her in a slow dance by the water. Their feet sank into the cool sand, their hearts beating as one beneath the starlit sky.

When the festivities wound down, the couple bid their guests goodnight, following a lantern-lit path to the cottage.

At the threshold, Blake did what any man in love would do—he swept Ray into his arms.

Laughter bubbled between them as he carried her onto the patio, where candles flickered in the warm night breeze, casting shadows that danced like fireflies.

And then he took her into his arms and waltzed her across the patio until both were breathless, drunk on love and the magic of the night.

Ray led him into their room, marveling at how Aria had transformed the space.

"She has that special touch," she murmured.

Blake, however, had eyes only for her. He cupped her face, his voice quiet but firm.

"Come here, Ray. I want to anchor in your heart. My love, this night will be a bonding of mind, soul, and body. You have been in my dreams forever, and now we'll join together for the rest of our lives. May our Father in Heaven bless our union."

Ray smiled, kissed his fingertips, and led their faithful dog, Journey, to the living room before closing the bedroom door behind her.

She paused at the window, looking up at the sliver of a moon. A fingernail moon—new beginnings.

Ray slowly opened her eyes to the gentle morning light coming through the window and immediately heard Journey's whine. She wondered what time it was. Blake stirred, but she didn't want to wake him. Quietly, she slipped out of bed, shutting the bedroom door behind her.

Journey nearly tackled her in his excitement.

"Hey, sweet boy. I'm sorry we didn't include you last night," she chuckled, scratching behind his ears. "I'm sure you're eager to stretch your legs. Go on, have a short romp. I'll have your breakfast ready when you get back."

As he bounded outside, Ray made her way to the kitchen, the scent of fresh coffee filling the air. She poured herself a cup, adding a generous amount of heavy cream, then stepped out onto the porch.

Journey was already racing through the shallow surf, his golden fur glistening in the morning light.

Before he ate, he rested his head in her lap and let out a small whine.

Ray smiled, running her fingers through his fur. "Good boy, Journey. I love you too, big fella."

She took a sip of her coffee—bold, rich, and creamy. The waves were calm, the sky an endless blue.

Her heart swelled.

Last night had been unlike anything she had imagined. At forty-seven, she had given herself to a man for the first time, and it had been more than just a physical experience. It had been a merging of two souls, a sacred communion designed by God Himself.

Blake had discovered the truth on his own, and instead of making her feel inexperienced, he had cherished her. He had been tender, patient, knowing exactly how to bring her pleasure in ways that touched not just her body, but her spirit.

"Thank You, Heavenly Father," she whispered.

The front door creaked open behind her.

"Good morning, my beautiful wife."

Ray turned, smiling. "Hello, my sweet man. How do you feel this morning?"

Blake stretched, his grin wide. "Like I'm twenty-one instead of fifty-five!"

Ray laughed. "Oh, but you have the wisdom of someone much older than twenty-one. And I adore who you are—your spirit, your tenderness. I'm glad I waited for God's timing. I'm glad I waited for you."

Blake reached for her hand, his expression soft. "All I can say is…I'm speechless."

And for a man who had spent his life with words, that said everything.

Chapter Sixteen

The last leg of Rihard's journey was finally here. As the plane descended toward the Cayman Islands, he pressed his forehead against the window, watching as the crystal-blue waters stretched endlessly below. He had spent weeks preparing for this moment, yet his heart still wrestled with a mix of excitement and fear.

Would they accept him? Would his art be as meaningful to them as it was to him? Would they see past the brushstrokes and into the soul of his work?

It had been an emotional whirlwind. His mother's passing still weighed heavily on him, a sorrow so deep that even the beauty of the Caribbean sky could not completely lift it. He regretted not finding his older brother in time—the one missing piece of his family. For years, he had searched, following leads that led to nowhere, only to be told that the adoption records had been sealed.

He and his mother had finally surrendered the search to God.

And now, there was nothing left for him in Latvia. No reason to return. No family, no home, just a chapter of his life that had ended. He had said farewell to a handful of casual friends, given away his mother's belongings, and returned the apartment key to the landlord.

As the plane touched down, he exhaled.

This was his fresh start.

Rihards had always believed that God revealed His glory through art.

Painting was not just a skill; it was his connection to the divine. Every brushstroke was an act of faith, a reflection of the miracles he had witnessed—some grand, some quiet, but all undeniable.

He recited Proverbs 3:5-6 in his mind:

"Do not trust your own understanding, but in all ways submit to God, and He will make your path straight."

It had always been true in his life. Even when doors had closed, even when it seemed impossible, God had made a way.

Like when his dream of studying at the Art Academy of Latvia had seemed out of reach.

He and his mother had scraped together enough money for two semesters. It wasn't much, but it was a start. And then, miraculously, a scholarship came. With it, he received housing and a food allowance, carrying him through until he completed his degree.

But at what cost?

He had rarely seen his mother in those last three years of school. She had sacrificed so much for him. And now, looking back, he wished he had been more attentive, more present.

Regret was a heavy thing to carry.

Yet, he knew God worked all things for good.

It had all started with a gamble.

With the little money he had saved, he had shipped a few of his paintings to various galleries in the U.S., hoping—praying—that someone would take notice.

He hadn't expected anything.

But then, an invitation had arrived.

A gallery in Naples, Florida, wanted to exhibit his work. And it was there that Mr. Forsyth had seen his paintings and extended an offer beyond his imagination.

Now, here he was.

Standing in an airport in a foreign place, surrounded by strangers, yet somehow, he knew this was exactly where he was meant to be.

God's plan was unfolding.

He closed his eyes for a moment, whispering a prayer:

Dear Father in Heaven, You've brought me through so many valleys, and I am thankful. I've never asked for much and expected even less. But now, dear Father, I am asking You—help me to connect with people through the talent You've given me.

And Father...

I've never even had a girlfriend.

He smiled slightly at the thought, feeling a bit foolish.

So I'm asking You... guide me on the path where I might meet someone of Your choosing, someone who will walk this journey of faith with me. One day, if it is Your will, I would love to have a family of my own.

Amen.

As he stepped forward to claim his luggage, he had no idea that his life was about to change forever.

Chapter Seventeen

Sid and Blake stood together at the airport, waiting for Rihards. The plane had landed, and passengers were making their way to baggage claim. Sid held a small, printed sign that said, 'Welcome Rihards!'

A young man in jeans and a t-shirt walked up to them and extended his hand. "Hi, I am Rihards."

Blake spoke enthusiastically, "Rihards, we are so excited to have you visit us! My name is Blake, and my friend here is Sid. Let us help you with your luggage."

Rihards smiled slightly and shook his head. "Thanks. I only have one small suitcase, and I believe I see it. I'll grab it and be right back."

Blake and Sid exchanged glances. There was something solemn and distant about the young man—not unkind, just guarded.

As the three men situated themselves in the car, Blake told Rihards all about the new gallery.

"We've got a beautiful space ready, and we'd love to feature your work."

Rihards hesitated before responding.

"Blake, I am sorry to disappoint, but I have not been able to paint since returning home. I laid my mom to rest and visited with old acquaintances. I don't have any family, so there remains nothing for me in Latvia anymore."

Blake quietly responded, "No need to apologize; we are deeply sorry about your mother. If there is anything at all we can do, please let us know."

Sid spoke up, "Rihards, you will be staying with me at our villa. Blake is a newlywed and resides with his new bride in her cottage on the beach. The villa has plenty of room for you to set up a studio and begin painting when you are inspired to do so."

At that, Rihards straightened. His eyes, distant moments ago, now held a flicker of resolve. "I want to start knocking out canvases right away. I have so much bottled up in my heart to express, and I've never been much of a talker, so the canvas allows me to speak."

Blake said, "Rihards, as soon as you get settled in the villa, I want you to come have dinner with us at the cottage. My wife, Ray, would like to meet you. She has worked very hard to make our gallery a place for artists to shine."

A genuine smile crossed Rihards' face. "That sounds so welcoming. I want to see the gallery soon, but for now, if it is okay with you and Sid, I would like some quiet time at the villa to gather my thoughts and start producing paintings worthy of your investment. I do not want to disappoint nor take advantage of either of you, gentlemen. I know God has given me a talent for placing on canvas what He has inscribed on my heart, so just be patient for a week. That is all I ask."

"Of course, Rihards, that sounds perfect to me. We have ten days before the grand opening. No pressure, okay? Just paint as your heart leads," Blake said.

Sid said, "I hope you are not expecting a five-star chef because I am not, but I promise you'll enjoy the fresh fare of the island. I'll make sure you are comfortable but also give you space of your own. I know the beautiful sunsets here in Cayman will bring peace to your spirit and inspire you to paint what God has laid on your heart."

As Blake pulled up to the villa and helped unload Rihards' suitcase, his mind wandered. There was something about Rihards that reminded him of himself. His bond with his mother. The loneliness of losing her. The weight of an uncertain future.

And then, his thoughts drifted to Rachel.

Would she carry the same unbearable emptiness when his time came?

He had done his best to shield her from it—to give her joy in the present rather than burden her with the future. But was that the right choice?

Would she one day resent him for not allowing her to grieve while he was still here?

Blake shook off the thoughts and smiled as Rihards gave a small nod of gratitude before stepping inside the villa.

There was time for all of it.

For grief.

For healing.

And, for new beginnings.

Chapter Eighteen

Ray had anticipated meeting Rihards and was a little disappointed that he would need quiet time at the villa a week or so before introductions. But as usual, her disappointment lasted only a brief time, and she went forward with an acute awareness of God's direction and blessings.

The weather was spectacular in every way. A cool breeze and the slant of sun rays told her that fall would be ushered in soon. Living in Cayman, one rarely experienced signs of the four seasons other than the change in ocean waves and the sun's position.

Nevertheless, this time of year, she always planted vegetables in her garden that would thrive in fall weather. Old habits die hard. Her mind darted back to living in Pakistan in the Hunza Valley. She loved the wonderful food that was grown in the fertile valley. She longed for the smell of rich dirt that produced a gardener's delight: the texture, weight, and balanced moisture produced beautiful rows of gorgeous vegetation. For a moment, she wondered about Simon and his beautiful son.

Lord, am I too old to have a child?

She knew the answer might not be simple. With Blake's health, his heart, their future together... maybe carrying a child wasn't meant to be. But still, she let herself wonder.

Just for a moment.

"Journey! Come on, boy. Let's run on the beach and explore. We may find treasures!"

Back home from the gallery, Blake sat at his desk, sketching out ideas for the grand opening. He needed Ray's creativity—her eye for detail, her way of making something ordinary feel extraordinary.

But she wasn't home.

And he realized something surprising: he missed her presence.

Not just her words or her ideas—just her.

Since their marriage, he'd found peace in the silences they shared, the casual conversations, the way her spirit filled their home without effort.

Blake set his pen down, leaned back, and closed his eyes.

For the first time in a long time, exhaustion wrapped around him like a heavy quilt.

Later in the afternoon, Ray and Journey returned to find Blake asleep in the bedroom.

She peered in, watching him sleep.

So deeply.

So soundly.

A small, nagging thought tugged at her—was he more tired than usual? But she pushed it away, unwilling to let fear creep into a perfect day.

Instead, she brewed coffee, grabbed a chew bone for Journey, and nestled into her favorite rocker outside, feet buried in the silky flour-like sand.

She let the waves lull her into God's peace.

The door opened, and she looked up to find Blake's twinkling eyes.

His white hair, sun-kissed skin, and that smile— he didn't look a day over forty.

"Greetings, my beautiful wife. I've missed you today."

He bent down and tenderly kissed her full on the lips. She could not help noticing that he looked a little tired. He sat down in the rocker beside her. Journey placed his head in Blake's lap and whined.

"Journey, what's that whine about, boy?" Blake asked.

"Darling, are you feeling okay? You usually do not take an afternoon nap."

"You are right, but when I came in from the gallery, I fell into bed and went into a deep sleep."

Ray reached for his hand, lacing her fingers through his. "Perhaps we should be lazy tomorrow, and I'll prepare a picnic lunch. The weather is perfect for spreading a blanket in the shade by the koi pool. We can just be at ease and enjoy relaxing and napping together. Doesn't that sound blissful?"

"It's a date, my love," whispered Blake.

Ray squeezed his hand, willing away the unease in her heart.

Tomorrow would be a day of rest.

And maybe, just maybe, they both needed it more than they realized.

Chapter Nineteen

The day of the gallery's grand opening had arrived. Rihards' exhibit demanding his presence was scheduled for 5 p.m. He had been faithful to his commitment to completing additional canvases for the exhibit. He was particularly excited about a painting that would be unveiled. It would be a surprise to everyone but Sid. Sid was his partner in crime in this little scheme!

Since he arrived, Sid had only been the constant companion and the humble servant. He was looking forward to seeing Blake again and meeting Ray at the opening. Sid had shown him pictures he had taken of the gallery, and it could not have been more well-appointed. Rihards could not imagine why Blake had invested so much time and money promoting him, but he was grateful and honored.

Sid had purchased a beautiful, long-sleeved, white silk shirt for Rihards to wear with a pair of jeans he had brought.

The jeans were unique with white stitching and paired with the shirt perfectly.

Sid also mentioned that Ray would display some of her newly framed photographs at the opening. Rihards was curious about this creative woman in her late forties who had recently married for the first time.

The banter of conversation between Sid and Rihards was infrequent. Sid did not want to intrude as he knew Rihards needed time to grieve, to paint, and to heal. What Sid witnessed, though, was a man of determination, strength, and talent. He was truly a gift from the Lord.

Sid called to Rihards, "Are you ready to depart for the Treasure Trove Gallery?"

"Yes, and I like the name of the gallery. Very appropriate for the island, don't you think?"

"I do. People come from many places to scuba dive here and seem to love all the treasures they discover from the sea. We're going to test their eyes tonight on spotting a genius at work. You have a God-given talent Rihards, and I believe your art will sell well and quickly."

"I hope Blake has not priced my work out of reach."

"I hope he has priced it high enough to make the sale worthy of you, Rihards."

Rihards blushed and followed Sid to the car.

The Treasure Trove Gallery parking lot had already filled to capacity. Sid circled around and finally parked two blocks from the gallery.

Blake and Ray were busy serving punch to all the visitors as they walked through viewing the artistic displays. The lighting enhanced every painting and photograph. Ray had paid close attention to trying to establish natural light to bring the subjects to life. In the center of the front open area was an easel with a beautiful crimson drape covering a large painting. The small sign attached read: The finale unveiling at 10 p.m.

Sid and Rihards strolled through the front doors, and there was a hush over the crowd. Blake approached them and shook hands, then guided Rihards to front and center.

"Ladies and gentlemen, I want to introduce Rihards Giddings. Rihards is the first artist to display his canvases in our gallery. We searched for this young man because we knew that such a talent did not need to remain silent in the background. His paintings will be known worldwide in a very short time. For years, my profession has been purchasing artwork that was unique and profitable, but now that I'm retired, I just want to promote an individual who deserves to reveal his God-given talent and allow art enthusiasts to enjoy his paintings in their homes and share with their loved ones. Please, everyone, come meet Rihards and feel free to ask questions about his work."

As the crowd slowly dispersed, Ray approached him.

She extended her hand, her grip small but firm, steady but warm.

And then—their eyes met.

For a brief, strange moment, time seemed to pause.

Ray's expression shifted—not just curiosity, not just admiration. There was something deeper, something recognition-like.

She hesitated.

Rihards waited.

And then, as if breaking free from an invisible hold, Ray smiled. "Rihards, I'm so happy to finally meet you. I've heard so much about you and your incredible gift."

Rihards exhaled, returning her smile. "Thank you, Ray. It's an honor to be here. And I must say, I admire your photography. You have a way of capturing life—not just moments, but life itself."

A soft flush of appreciation crossed Ray's face. "That's very kind of you. Blake and I would love to have you over sometime soon. We'll make it happen."

"I'd like that," Rihards said sincerely.

Ray nodded and stepped aside, allowing others to meet him. But as she walked away, her fingers grazed the back of her neck—a nervous habit.

Something about Rihards unsettled her.

Something familiar.

The night carried on with laughter, conversation, and sales. Rihards watched as art collectors discussed his work, pulling out their checkbooks, pointing at the brushstrokes, making quiet, reverent remarks. He had never experienced this kind of validation before.

Then, as the clock neared ten, Blake took center stage once again.

"Before we close for the evening, I want to invite Rihards to join me for a special unveiling."

All eyes turned to the large crimson-draped canvas at the front of the room.

Rihards stepped forward, hands at his sides, his heartbeat calm but expectant.

Sid, standing near the back, gave him a discreet nod.

With one smooth pull, the crimson drape fell away.

The room fell silent.

Then—gasps.

And then—applause.

But Rihards wasn't looking at the crowd.

His eyes were on Ray and Blake.

Ray stood frozen, her hands covering her mouth, tears slipping silently down her cheeks.

Blake blinked rapidly, his arm instinctively wrapping around his wife.

The painting before them was breathtaking.

A sunset so magnificent it seemed to glow from within stretched across the canvas, a wash of gold and amber cascading into deep ocean blues.

And at the center—Ray and Blake, standing at the shoreline, their bodies wrapped in the delicate embrace of the wind.

Ray's wedding gown swayed with the ocean breeze, curling slightly around Blake's legs. Their hands were intertwined, their foreheads almost touching—a moment of love and devotion frozen in time.

Rihards finally spoke.

"Our friend, Sid, helped me acquire a photograph from a young lady named Aria. She took pictures at your wedding. This painting is my gift to you both—a thank you."

A hush settled once more, but this time, it was not out of surprise.

It was reverence.

Blake cleared his throat, fighting emotion. "Rihards... this is—" He stopped, shaking his head. There were no words.

Ray took a slow step forward, studying the painting, her fingers trembling.

And then, with quiet sincerity, she whispered, "It's perfect."

As the evening wrapped up, Blake addressed the guests one final time.

"This evening has been one of the highlights of my life." His voice was steady, though his eyes were still glassy. "I must thank my lovely wife, Ray. Her vision brought this gallery to life. And please, for those of you who purchased her photography tonight—know that you have a treasure."

A round of applause followed.

Guests slowly made their way out, hands filled with newly acquired art, hearts filled with something even greater.

Sid clapped a hand on Rihards' shoulder. "You did well, my friend. Very well."

Rihards exhaled, looking around at what had unfolded— the success, the emotion, the purpose in every brushstroke.

For the first time in a long time, he felt something new.

Peace.

And maybe—just maybe—he had finally found a place to belong.

Chapter Twenty

The morning sun rays danced across the bed as the branches from the mango tree were tossed about by the strong ocean breeze. Ray looked over to see a smile on Blake's peaceful face as he slept deeply. She thought about the previous evening's events and felt unsettled in her emotions. She could not put her finger on it, but something was causing a stir in her soul. She quietly arose from the bed and headed for the kitchen.

"Hey, Journey! Ready to go out, boy?"

She opened the front door for him. As she looked out toward the ocean, something stirred in her soul and her memory again.

Those eyes.

Rihards' eyes.

They were Byron's eyes.

She had spent the whole morning trying to rationalize the resemblance, trying to dismiss it as coincidence. But no matter how she turned it over in her mind, the possibility remained.

Could Byron have had a brother? A twin?

She made herself a cup of coffee and sat in the rocker as Journey ate his breakfast beside her. She stroked his beautiful fur and told him she loved him. The minutes became an hour as she pondered the things in her heart. *Dear Lord, could it be? Could this young man be looking for his brother? Is that why he is in the States? Oh, Lord, our journeys are so very interwoven with others. We are all connected. You designed it that way. All I ask from you, dear Jesus, is that YOU be with me. That's all I ask. Amen.*

Blake poked his head out the door and smiled. "Darling, whatever is the matter? You are pale as though you've seen a ghost."

Ray swallowed, steadying her voice. "Sweetheart, would you pour yourself a cup of coffee and come sit with me? I want to ask you some questions."

"Of course. Be right back."

Blake disappeared inside for a moment, returning with his coffee. He sat beside her, his fingers wrapping around the warm mug. "Alright, tell me what's on your mind."

"Where is Rihards from?"

"His family is from Latvia, but I believe he has been in the States for a while."

Ray felt her heart skip a beat.

She placed her hands in her lap, suddenly aware of how tightly she was gripping them together.

"My adopted son, Byron, was from Latvia."

"Well, that's a coincidence."

"No, Blake, you are wrong. This is not a coincidence. I believe God placed Rihards in our path for a reason. He may have been looking for Byron. That could have been why he is in America. He favors Byron; as a matter of fact, they could almost be twins."

"Ray, you only mentioned your son, who died, briefly, and I'm not sure Latvia was mentioned. This is unbelievable. I remember your saying you stumbled upon an orphanage during a tour with the Peace Corps, and you stayed for a year in order to complete the adoption requirements before traveling back to America with your son."

"That's correct."

"Well, we know that Rihards' mother recently died, so it seems he would be the only one who could share details about his family or siblings. Let's have a quick breakfast, and I'll ride over to the villa and ask Rihards to come here for a visit. How does that sound?"

"Thank you. I would love to speak with him and learn the truth."

Soon, she would have answers.

And she wasn't sure whether she was ready for them… or terrified of what they might reveal.

Chapter Twenty-One

Ray showered and dressed in a pink t-shirt and white shorts. Her legs were tan and firm in her shorts. She had been active all her life, and her shape was still the same as when she was in her teens. Her auburn hair was highlighted with platinum streaks. She had never used color to disguise her age. Age to Ray was only a matter of the heart. She had a few light brown freckles scantily sprinkled across her nose, and her enormous hazel eyes looked as if she had always anticipated a pleasant surprise right around the corner. She spread pink gloss on her lips and walked out the front door just in time to greet Rihards as he and Blake pulled up in the driveway.

"Good morning, Rihards. I'm so happy you came to visit us! Let's go out on the patio. I prepared some fresh fruit and blueberry scones. I think you'll enjoy our backyard area."

When Rihards stepped out onto the patio and gazed around, he was taken aback by the little paradise. "This place is incredible. You, indeed, are a professional gardener. What an awakening to one's senses! The smell of rich earth, the koi peacefully gliding around lily pads, and the wafting fragrance of a blossom of some description. All I can say is: this is paradise."

Ray laughed at his description of their place. "Rihards, I feel the exact same way, but I have probably never expressed my thoughts the way you just did. Blake and I spend many relaxing hours out here. When the moonflowers bloom at night, this place is enchanting, especially with a full moon. You'll have to visit us one evening. As a matter of fact, we should have you and Aria over for dinner soon. I believe you and Aria are probably close to the same age. She is a designer. Plus, she was born on the island, so she has a wealth of knowledge about the history of the Cayman Islands."

Rihards asked, "Wasn't she present at the grand opening? Seems like I remember seeing a young woman busy serving and talking with clients."

"Yes, that was Aria. She lives in a bungalow on the beach within walking distance of us."

Blake brought iced tea on a tray and placed it on the patio table. "I don't know about you guys, but I'm still sleepy. I hope this caffeine places a dance in my step! Rihards, please have a seat. These blueberry scones are just out of the oven, so help yourself."

As they relaxed, Rihards studied Ray carefully, his expression shifting.

"Ray, I need to ask… Have we met before?"

Ray's heart skipped.

"I don't think so," she answered slowly. "But… I did live in Latvia for over a year."

Rihards exhaled sharply. "I have a picture of my older brother with a woman who looks exactly like you."

Ray felt her pulse quicken. "Where did you get the picture?"

"An adoption agency."

The words sent a jolt through her.

"An adoption agency?" she repeated, barely above a whisper.

Rihards nodded. "I had an older brother—he was placed in an orphanage as a baby because our mother was a drug addict. She wasn't fit to care for him. This was before I was born. When I was a teenager, my mother and I tried to find him, but the records were sealed. We were only told he was adopted, safe, and well cared for."

He swallowed, his eyes locking onto hers. "Before I left, the agency worker gave me a picture. A picture of my brother and his adoptive mother."

His voice softened, almost hesitant.

"You're the woman in the picture, aren't you, Ray?"

The world tilted slightly.

Ray reached for Blake's hand beneath the table, her fingers trembling. "I am."

Rihards sucked in a breath. "Then Byron was my brother."

The name hung in the air, heavy and full of unspoken loss.

Ray nodded, her voice breaking. "Yes."

Rihards' jaw tightened. "When can I see him?"

Ray's heart splintered.

"Rihards… Byron passed away."

Silence.

Then, tears slipped down Rihards' face. He didn't wipe them away. He just sat there, breathing, absorbing.

Ray reached across and took his hand. "But he was loved. He was so, so loved."

Walks, Memories, and Healing

The beach stretched before them, golden and endless, as Ray and Rihards walked side by side. They walked for miles, their feet sinking into the warm sand, their words weaving a story of loss, love, and fate.

Ray told him everything. About Byron's love for Montana's mountains, his laughter, his kindness.

Rihards listened, taking it all in like a man grasping onto the last echoes of someone he never got to know.

They cried at different times, their grief a shared thread in an unfinished tapestry.

By the time they returned, something had shifted.

Ray had lost a son.

Rihards had lost a brother.

But somehow, through the pain, they had found a piece of each other.

When Ray and Rihards returned to the cottage, Blake was napping. Ray invited Rihards in for dinner, but he declined and asked her to drive him back to the villa where Sid would have dinner prepared.

The two of them had walked at least five miles on the beach, and she answered all the questions Rihards had asked about Byron. Rihards had the same easy-going way and kind spirit. When she had first related that Byron was dead, Rihards was silent, and then tears rolled down his cheeks. But as she continued to share Byron's life experiences in Montana, Rihards reveled in hearing all about his brother.

When she saw Blake sleeping, she stopped in her tracks. She knew.

She could see it in the way he tired so easily, the way his energy flickered like a candle in the wind.

Still, when she returned from taking Rihards back to the villa, Blake had rallied.

"Hello, beautiful. I hope smoked salmon and stir-fried garden vegetables sound good tonight."

Ray's throat tightened. He was always taking care of her.

She kissed him softly. "Sounds perfect. Let's eat outside and watch the moonflowers open. As a matter of fact, I found several comforters in the linen closet and placed them by the koi pool so we could sleep outside."

During their meal, Ray related the conversation that she and Rihards had, and Blake mentioned that maybe Rihards could have a home base on the island. They spoke of introducing Aria to Rihards and building an addition to the gallery so Rihards could set up a small studio. After dinner and non-stop conversation, Ray went inside, slipped into her pajamas and grabbed two pillows and a large throw.

Before they bedded down, Blake turned on the CD player and they waltzed to instrumental music until both were breathless.

"Blake, come lie down beside me. Just look at that sky. It is full of hidden secrets that have mystified man since the beginning of time. Impossible to count the stars and comprehend a Creator who spoke the universe into existence, is it not?"

Blake pulled her very close and held her against his chest. His heartbeat.

The ocean's song.
The smell of salt and moonflowers.
Ray memorized it all.
She knew time was precious.
She would hold onto this moment for as long as she could.

Chapter Twenty-Two

The salty air carried the scent of sun-warmed sand and hibiscus as the islands stirred with new life. November was approaching, and tourists descended upon the islands like flocks of geese from the north. Many people who resided in areas with bitter winters would spend several months on the islands starting in November. This was the time profits were realized for their little community.

Rihards, having poured his heart into his work, had completed six new masterpieces. His brushstrokes held the weight of his grief, his healing, and his rediscovery of purpose. Each painting told a story. During the grand opening, his works had sold for a combined $39,000, and now, with growing recognition from word of mouth and magazine features, his paintings commanded prices of $12,000 to $15,000 each.

Saxton had taken note of Rihards' growing influence and added a studio space within the gallery. A glass panel separated the studio from the gallery; many customers loved to watch the canvases come to life.

One particular onlooker never seemed to tire of watching him—Aria.

She was mesmerized by Rihards' talent. She envisioned him doing more with his talent than painting on canvas.

But she didn't just admire his work; she saw potential beyond the canvas.

One evening, as they strolled the beach at sunset, the water lapping at their feet, Aria shared an idea.

"Your talent shouldn't be limited to paintings alone," she mused. "We should create something truly unique—a shop filled with one-of-a-kind art pieces. Something no one else can duplicate."

Rihards had merely smiled. It was the first time in months he had entertained the idea of the future.

Their evening walks became a quiet tradition. She walked with him through his grief, offering companionship without expectation. She understood the weight of loss, the way it lingered even in the most beautiful moments.

Sid had mentioned to Ray that he was going to depart for Scotland soon, but his voice carried an unspoken concern.

"Ray... Blake doesn't look well."

Ray's stomach clenched, but she nodded. "I know."

Blake was fiercely private about his health. He never complained, never sought sympathy, never let on when something was wrong. But Ray had always been able to read between the silences.

For now, she chose not to press him.

But deep in her heart, she knew.

On this particular afternoon, just two months after Ray and Blake were married, Ray was running with Journey on the beach when she felt a very sharp pain in her lower abdomen. She slowed down to a walk and then sat on the sand, hugging her knees close to her chest.

Dear Lord, help me to know what is going on. Place Your healing touch on my body and give me Your wisdom to help me discern what is happening.

A thought drifted through her mind—so obvious, so natural, she couldn't believe she hadn't considered it sooner.

Could she be pregnant?

The realization sent a thrill through her chest, unlike anything she had felt in years. Hope surged within her.

She would wait two weeks before telling Blake. Not out of secrecy, but out of caution. She needed to be sure.

She whistled to Journey. "Let's go home, boy!" She had not been this excited since she adopted Byron.

The moment Ray stepped inside, Blake's gaze locked onto her.

"What?" he asked, his eyes narrowing slightly.

Ray blinked. "What do you mean, what?"

Blake studied her face, then smiled knowingly. "Let me see if I can describe your expression… There's a sparkle in those big hazel eyes. A secret you're barely containing. Anticipation. So, tell me—what's up?"

She laughed, shaking her head in disbelief. "Wow. How do you know me so well in such a short time?"

Blake pulled her into his arms, his voice a whisper against her ear. "Because we are joined together, and our hearts beat as one."

Her breath caught.

She had planned to wait.

But how could she keep this from him when he already felt it in his soul?

"I was going to wait a little longer before sharing," she admitted, "but since you must know..." She took his hand and placed it over her still-flat stomach. "I think we're going to have a child."

Blake's breath hitched.

For a long moment, he simply held her, stroking her hair. When he finally spoke, his voice was thick with emotion.

"Since I fell in love with you, I've wondered if God might bless us with a child. I never mentioned it, never wanted to place that expectation on us. But my heart wouldn't let go of the thought. Is that what you want too, my darling wife?"

Ray's eyes filled with tears. "After Byron, I never imagined having another child. But now... now, I feel like God is giving us a new beginning."

Blake pressed her hand to his chest. "Feel that?"

His heartbeat thundered beneath her palm.

"Sweetheart, this is a true gift from God. Let's go forward with no doubts, no fear—only joy. Let's rejoice and plan for this little one."

He kissed her deeply, with all the love and devotion in his soul.

Then he whispered, "Now, there are three hearts that beat as one. Come lie down with me, and let's hold one another."

She walked into the bedroom, stepped out of her clothes, and slid under the crisp, clean sheets. Blake shut the door. Journey whined and then settled down in the living room.

Chapter Twenty-Three

When Ray awakened in the mornings, her mind started traveling forward, always forward. Before placing her feet on the floor, she would look over to make sure Blake was okay and sleeping peacefully. Then, she would give herself and her day to God to mark the course for her and let her live an unhurried life.

Christmas was only a week away, and there were many things not yet checked on the to-do list. She reminded herself that letting everything unfold as God wished was alright.

Dear Lord, I have a request for You on behalf of Blake. Please help Rachel's heart to be tender toward her dad. He patiently waits for her to reply that she will join us for Christmas. Please let it be, Lord, if it is Your will.

She eased out of the bed and grabbed her robe. Journey was beginning to whimper at the door. When she opened the door to let him out, she spotted Rihards standing in the driveway.

He lifted a hand in greeting, and she motioned for him to come inside.

She tied her robe and started coffee in the kitchen. She started preparing fresh fruit and heard Rihards in the living room. When she walked in, she was astonished at what she saw. Rihards had set up two easels with Christmas paintings displayed. One was the most perfect Santa Claus you could imagine from a child's imagination. The other was a simple snow scene with a red cardinal on a mailbox and beautiful evergreens flocked by white, fluffy snow drifts in the background. Both would sell quickly.

Ray pressed a hand to her chest. "Rihards... these are exquisite."

He smiled softly. "They are not for the gallery, Ray. They are for you."

She turned to him, confused. "For me?"

He nodded. "Santa Claus is a tribute to Byron, to celebrate the childlike spirit that still lived inside him, even after all he had endured. He didn't have much of a childhood, but you—you gave him love, protection, and a place to belong."

Ray's vision blurred as tears welled in her eyes.

"And the cardinal?" she whispered.

"The redbird is a reminder of the blood Jesus shed for us, and the snow... a symbol of the pure heart He calls us to have. The subjects of these paintings have been in my heart for a long time, but I could never bring myself to paint them until now.

"Ray... Blake... Sid... Aria... You have been a healing balm to my broken spirit. These paintings are just a small token of the love I carry for all of you. Thank you."

Ray's breath hitched.

Then, without warning, she broke.

The emotions she had been holding in for so long—the grief she had locked away, the sorrow she had never fully allowed herself to feel—came rushing out in uncontrollable sobs.

Blake rushed in from the bedroom, alarm flashing across his face. Without hesitation, he wrapped her in his arms, his hands running up and down her back in soothing strokes.

Across the room, Rihards sat down heavily on the sofa, his own shoulders shaking with silent tears.

For a few moments, the room was filled with nothing but the sounds of weeping and love unspoken.

After Ray explained the emotional commotion to Blake, with the assistance of Rihards, they all gathered on the patio for coffee and breakfast. The three of them normally had breakfast together a couple of times a week.

Ray confessed, "I was never able to let myself truly grieve over Byron. This was the first time I've fallen apart since his death."

Blake held her small hand. "Then this morning was long overdue."

"Yes, and perhaps the emotions I'm feeling as we expect our child may have given me permission."

Rihards' look of surprise was priceless, and everyone started laughing.

"Ray! You're having another son?" he exclaimed. "That means I'll have a little brother!"

Blake chuckled. "Or a little sister."

Rihards shrugged, grinning. "Either way, they're going to be so spoiled." He sobered slightly. "It doesn't matter, boy or girl—just that the baby is healthy and that you're okay, Ray."

Blake nodded in agreement. "My exact thoughts."

As the waves whispered along the shore, Ray lifted her eyes to the sky, feeling something she had not felt in a long time.

Peace.

And for the first time since Byron's passing, she let it in.

Chapter Twenty-Four

The night sky was breathtaking—stars shimmering like scattered diamonds, and the moon hung low, glowing with a delicate pink hue.

Aria tilted her head, eyes full of wonder. "I've never seen the night sky more beautiful. And look at that moon! Doesn't its soft glow remind you of the moonflower blooms? They reveal themselves only to the night, offering their sweet fragrance to our Creator."

Blake replied to Aria, "Thanks for bringing my attention to our Creator's sky art. Yes, this awesome moon tonight brings one's attention to the Creation and our majestic Creator. I realize how insignificant we are in many ways, but when I think that God created man to have dominion over the Earth, it helps me see how much He loves us."

Ray and Rihards were busy transporting food to the patio area as Blake and Aria relaxed and conversed. Rihards had made himself at home in the kitchen, and Ray loved it!

Ray glanced over at her husband, who had been quiet the past two days. She knew why. Rachel had declined their Christmas invitation. Blake hadn't pressed the issue, but Ray could see the sadness in his eyes.

Pushing aside the thought, she called out, "This is the last trip from the kitchen! Let's sit, bless this food, and eat. I'm starving—but these days, when am I not?"

Blake led them in prayer, and soon, laughter and conversation filled the air.

As Rihards and Aria prepared to leave, Blake asked them to stay a few more minutes, so he and Ray could share their news.

"We're building a larger cottage," Blake announced. "And we'd love to offer this place to you, Rihards. We can work out a low monthly rate—much lower than your villa lease. And look at what comes with it: all the fresh fruit and vegetables you can eat, a koi pool, and the most beautiful moonflowers."

A wide grin spread across Rihards' face. "This is an incredible offer... and I'd love to accept."

But then, he hesitated, glancing at Aria. "Actually, we have news too."

Ray gasped. "Well, out with it! Hurry! I can't wait!"

Rihards shifted nervously, then took Aria's hand. "I asked Aria to marry me... if she's willing to take a chance on an unknown artist."

The squeal that left Ray's lips could have woken the whole island. She and Blake rushed forward, pulling them into tight embraces.

Aria laughed. "I've been about to burst! I wanted to share earlier, but I was waiting for Rihards to take the lead."

Rihards turned to her, his voice thoughtful. "What if you sold your house, and we combined your earnings with my income, and…"

Aria raised a brow. "And what?"

Rihards turned to Ray and Blake. "Would you two consider selling rather than renting?"

Blake extended his hand immediately, shaking Rihards' firmly. "First, congratulations. You two remind me so much of Ray and me—when you know, you act, because life's too short to hesitate."

Ray hugged Aria tightly. "It would be such a blessing to sell this home to you two. Right, Blake?"

Blake nodded without hesitation. "Absolutely. We'll work out the details after Christmas. Sound good?"

Rihards' eyes shone. "Perfect. Is Sid coming back for Christmas?"

Blake exhaled. "We're not sure yet, but we do want you guys here for Christmas Eve."

"Wouldn't miss it."

As Rihards and Aria walked toward their car, he wrapped an arm around her, pulling her close. Love was in the air, and Christmas had never felt more magical.

Later that night, as Ray drifted into sleep in his arms, Blake lay awake, staring at the moon through the window.

It was one of those moments that stopped him in his tracks.

God, our Creator, could it get any better than to behold your creation with my wife and child held close to my body? May you always help me to recognize the quality of life in the present moment.

Yet, even as he prayed, he felt the weight of something pressing against his chest.

For the past two weeks, his breathing had become shallower. Maybe that explained why he had been sleeping more during the day.

He didn't want to dwell on it. There were too many good things happening.

As he closed his eyes, he made some mental notes. He would call Sid tomorrow and ask him to place his condo on the market. Fraserburgh real estate was booming, and his condo would bring in at least $800,000. He made another note to call his attorney and set up a trust fund for his child, who was yet to be born. The funds from the sale of the condo could be directly deposited in the trust, and Ray needed power of attorney, too.

Later, he would set up a trust for Rachel when he could determine an amount to be given to her. She had a healthy air of independence, and he did not know anything about her finances. Nevertheless, he would leave her money in a trust to draw from monthly, should she need it. He had worked smart over the years and only spent money when there was money to be made. Other than the villa he rented at Cayman each summer for the past few years, he had been very good at saving. He had probably accumulated close to $15,000,000, and his investments continued to produce dividends. Ray and their baby would have all their needs met. Ray, too, had been cautious about overspending. *Thank you, Lord, for ensuring that we are on the same page with our finances.*

He went over the important things once again that he had to do tomorrow. Just a few more things: call Saxton and request he meet with Ray about the plans for their new home, place $600,000 in an account for Saxton to draw from, and lastly, close the deal on the property he and Ray had seen last week and agreed on.

Lord, that's it for now. Would you please sing over us tonight and let us both sleep deeply and dream the dreams You've placed in our hearts? Amen.

With one final breath, he tightened his arms around Ray and closed his eyes.

And under the light of the moonflower moon, he surrendered to sleep, wrapped in love and grace.

Chapter Twenty-Five

Ray opened her eyes only slightly as the sun rays spilled across their bed. She wanted to keep them closed for just a little longer—to linger in the embrace of last night's memories. Christmas Eve had been nothing short of magical, with their loved ones gathered, laughter filling the cottage, and hearts rejoicing over the birth of their Savior. She breathed in deeply, her chest rising and falling in rhythm with the peace that settled over her.

There was so much to be grateful for. Blessings had come in waves over the past year, an unveiling and outpouring of God's gifts, one after another. Hot tears stung her eyes as emotion welled up within her. She pressed a hand over her heart, feeling its strong, steady rhythm.

Lord, You know my underlying concerns about Blake. I can tell he is growing weaker. Please help us through this journey. Show us that You are in control in all ways and carry us in Your blessed peace.

She turned her head slightly and studied Blake's sleeping form beside her. His chest rose and fell in a soothing cadence, his face peaceful in slumber. The golden morning light made his features even more striking—his strong jaw, the hint of a smile on his lips, the slight scruff that darkened his face. He was such a beautiful man.

Oh, God, let his rest be restorative. Let him wake renewed.

A soft whimper pulled her from her thoughts. Journey, their faithful golden retriever, stood near the bed, his tail wagging eagerly. She smiled and slipped from beneath the covers, careful not to disturb Blake. Quietly grabbing her swimsuit, she tiptoed from the room, closing the door gently behind her.

Ray had been so happy that Sid had flown in and celebrated with them. He had a growing concern for Blake but kept a guard over his mouth. He assured Blake that all legal concerns were taken care of in Scotland, and that pleased Blake immensely. Rihards was so happy to have Sid back at the villa as well. He seemed more inspired to paint with passion. Just this last week, two more paintings came forth on canvas, and both would quickly sell. People were beginning to fly to Cayman just to visit the gallery and purchase Rihards' paintings. Advertising was not something any of them needed to be intentional about anymore.

"Guess what, Journey? You and I are going for a swim this morning. I need to stretch and relax. Okay, boy, I know you are excited, but wait a moment, and let me put my swimsuit on!"

They ran like small children and splashed into the calm, warm water. The lemon-colored fish scattered under her feet, and some less shy, electric blue fish swam near her side. She always tried to reach out and gently touch their velvety bodies, but just as she would almost touch them, they would dart the other way. They were exquisite little creatures. She had looked on the internet to discover the names of the small, beautiful fish, and they were identified as the yellow longnose butterflyfish and the queen angelfish. These enchanting, exquisite swimmers always made her experience in the ocean magical! She lay there, floating in the water, allowing her mind to take her to another realm, when suddenly she felt strong arms pull her to an upright position.

"Blake!" she gasped, blinking water from her eyes.

"How could I miss a morning swim with you?" His voice was rich with amusement as he pulled her close.

She traced a hand over his shoulder. "I didn't hear you get up."

"I woke up missing you," he murmured before pressing a soft kiss to her lips.

She sighed against him, sinking into the warmth of his embrace. "Blake, did you know your lips are as soft as velvet?"

Laughing, he shook his head. "I was unaware of such a fact."

She playfully tapped his nose. "When you sleep in the mornings, it takes everything in me not to kiss you awake. You have a beautiful mouth."

His blue eyes darkened with affection. "Such secrets you've been keeping from me, my darling."

She grinned before tilting her face toward the sun. "Isn't it amazing how effortlessly one can float in these waters? There's no other place like it."

Blake followed her gaze, nodding. "You're right. Here, you can lie still and float forever. There's nowhere else I'd rather be."

They swam together, weightless and free, until their bellies rumbled in protest. Journey barked from the shore, wagging his tail as if calling them back.

Blake reached for her hand as they waded toward the beach. "Come on. I'm making breakfast for you this morning."

She laughed, shaking her head. "Blake, after all the Christmas cooking yesterday, I don't mind making breakfast."

"No," he insisted, squeezing her fingers. "You deserve a break."

Emotion swelled in her chest, and before she could stop herself, a tear slipped down her cheek. "Blake..." Her voice trembled. "I don't know what I would do without you. I love you so deeply. The thought of losing you—" She broke off, unable to finish.

Blake stopped walking and turned her toward him, cupping her face in his hands. His thumbs brushed away the tears as he searched her eyes.

"Hey," he murmured, his voice gentle yet firm. "Everything is going to be alright, I promise." He tucked a damp strand of hair behind her ear before kissing her forehead. "Now, where's that beautiful smile of yours?"

She inhaled shakily, blinking up at him.

For just a moment, he let his mind drift—he knew her heart's concerns, the constant thought that she may not have a husband much longer nor Max a father. His constant prayer was that the cascade of pure love that God had woven around his family and friends would be an eternal symphony, that would carry them and comfort them when he passed onto heaven. But for now in these precious moments, he would live to the fullest in the present blessings of Jesus, Who held all things together.

A smile spread across her beautiful face, all worries diminished. Both would live and revel in the moments God bestowed on them.

He grinned and tugged her along toward the cottage, the sound of their laughter mingling with the ocean breeze.

Chapter Twenty-Six

March arrived on the island, carried in by crisp, refreshing breezes. The air smelled of salt and blooming hibiscus, and Ray found immense joy in tending to her new garden. Since purchasing the property, she had carefully amended the soil, researched the best plants for the tropical climate, and ordered seeds and cuttings that would soon transform the space into a flourishing paradise.

Saxton, ever the watchful presence, worked tirelessly in the background. His careful eye followed her movements, making sure she didn't overwork herself in the sun. He had broken ground on the new home on the first of January, and the project was moving swiftly, thanks to his skilled and reliable crew.

She was tremendously grateful for Saxton. She had gotten to know him well in the last two years. He was around forty with a beautiful smile, thick black hair, and a gorgeous tan. Ray wondered why he had never married. Aria had told her several of the single women had tried to get to know him, but he was having none of it. Ray knew him to be a hardworking, dependable, and very kind individual.

Today, she was trying to keep up with the time and periodically would ask Saxton what time it was. Sid had asked her to visit with him at the villa. He had something confidential on his mind he wanted to discuss.

"Hey, Ray!" Saxton called out. "Don't let the time get by you."

"Oh, yes. Thanks Saxton. I'm leaving now. See you later."

"Sure thing."

She took her time walking to the villa. All the bending and stooping had caught up to her—a reminder that her body was changing. She placed a gentle hand on her stomach, smiling at the life growing within her. Perhaps the added blood volume of pregnancy was slowing her down just a bit. Still, she felt strong and capable, and she intended to keep up with everything that mattered to her.

Sid was sitting on the balcony and waved to her. She was going to run up the stairs but thought better of it and opted for the elevator instead.

"Have a seat, Ray. I already poured you a glass of homemade lemonade."

"Sid, this is the best!"

"I always have to put a twist of cherry in it!"

"So, tell me, what's on your mind?"

"In Hunza Valley, Pakistan, it is believed that one of the villagers has invented a serum that eradicates lung cancer. It seems that lung cancer is the only cancer the infusions are successful with. This serum cannot be shipped out of the country, but I'm told that cancer patients who travel there and have one infusion a week for five weeks are experiencing a cure."

Ray's heart pounded. "That is incredible, Sid."

"I know," he agreed. "But the problem is that the serum cannot be shipped out of the country. The only way to access it is to go there." He hesitated. "Do you think we could manage to convince Blake to go?"

"I'm not sure about that. You know as well as I do he does not feel the need for medical care."

"This serum is not exactly modern medicine. It is an extract from enzymes, herbs, and vitamin C. The real challenge is convincing Blake to leave the island for five weeks, and then there is the matter of lodging in Hunza Valley."

"Sid, I know someone there. If you got in touch with him, he would help with everything."

"You amaze me. Where have you not been?"

"Many places, but Hunza Valley is a paradise. I know a gentleman named Simon. I don't know that he has a phone, but there would be people in the community who could get a message to him. I'm confident he will help us."

"Please write down the facts as you know them, and I'll try to contact Simon and get as much information as possible before we broach Blake with this idea."

"Ok, Sid. We'll work through this together. Before presenting this to my husband, let's be thorough and secure accurate information. You know he can be just a tiny bit stubborn."

"Oh, do I know! Ray, I'll make some calls after I get the necessary information from you. I would be more than willing to accompany Blake to Pakistan and stay with him for five weeks."

"Sid, I don't think I could be away from Blake for five weeks!"

"Let's take this one step at a time. We're going to pray to our Heavenly Father for His guidance. After all, it is His plan, not ours."

"Yes, of course," Ray sighed and said no more.

A brief silence settled between them before Sid leaned back with a teasing grin. "I've not heard anyone mention if we are expecting a little girl or a little boy; what's the verdict?"

"We do not want to know ahead of time. All of us will find out at the same time when our healthy baby enters this world!"

"More anticipation, right?"

"Absolutely."

Sid lifted his glass. "Well then, here's to the future. Whatever it may hold."

Ray lifted hers in return. "To the future."

But as she clinked her glass against his, a single thought whispered in her mind—Would Blake agree to this journey, or was she grasping at a hope he would never reach for?

Chapter Twenty-Seven

The trip to the *Hard Rock Hunza Resort*, where Blake and Sid were staying, had been long and exhausting. The Jeep ride from Gilgit Airport had been particularly grueling, with winding mountain roads that seemed to stretch endlessly into the sky. The thin air at this altitude made every breath feel slightly heavier, a reminder that they were in a place unlike any other.

Sid leaned back against the cushioned chair in their suite, rubbing his face tiredly. His body ached, and exhaustion threatened to drag him under, but his eyes drifted toward Blake, who sat near the massive glass window, lost in thought. Hunza Valley stretched before them, a masterpiece of creation—towering snow-capped peaks, lush terraced fields, and rivers that shimmered under the early evening sun. There was an untouched, sacred beauty here, something that made a person feel small yet strangely whole.

"Blake, I'm going to place your luggage in the room that overlooks the valley, and I'll sleep in the back room," Sid said.

"Either one is fine with me. Stop for a moment and come sit here beside me. I was just imagining how Ray must have felt living here. Can you imagine the peace she must have found in this place? I'm sure it helped her through the grief after losing Byron. This valley…it feels like another world."

Sid nodded, stepping closer to the window. "Now, we understand what fueled her passion for photography. Blake, she is one of the most remarkable people I have ever met—gifted, wise, and full of love."

Blake exhaled, his fingers absently running over the wooden armrest of his chair. "I can hardly bear to think about being away from her, especially now. Our baby is so close to being born, and I feel this deep ache in my chest when I think of missing even a single moment."

Sid placed a reassuring hand on his friend's shoulder. "I promise—we will be back in time. You will hold your child in your arms, Blake. Do you have any feelings in your spirit regarding whether it will be a girl or a boy?" Sid asked.

"Yes. A son."

"I've thought the same, Blake."

"Did I give you the extra cell phone, Sid?"

"Yes. I'll collect it from my suitcase and have it handy for Simon when he arrives."

When Sid returned with the phone, he sat down again beside Blake. Both men remained silent and transfixed on the beauty that stretched miles and miles. The moment felt heavy with significance, as if the land itself whispered ancient secrets, urging them to trust the journey ahead.

Finally, Sid broke the silence and said, "Ray is one of the wisest individuals I have ever known. Can you believe a person she connected with years ago is helping us find our way on this journey?"

Blake stated with confidence, "Ray does the bidding of the Holy Spirit."

"You are right, my friend. I've witnessed this since the first time I met her. She is in the moment with the great 'I AM.'"

There was a knock at the door. "Please, Sid, would you get that while I rest?"

Sid answered the door. "Hello. You must be Simon?"

"Yes. That would be me."

"I'm Sid."

"Of course, Sid. I feel like I already know you from our communication over the last few weeks. How was your trip?"

"Our trip was fine: unremarkable and safe. Please come in and meet Blake, Ray's husband."

Simon extended his hand. "Very nice to meet you, Blake. And we are going to take very good care of you."

"Simon, Ray has filled me in on the history between the two of you. She and I both hope you and your family are safe and well."

"Thank you. We are all well and still together. We have had no more surprises from our government. My wife has managed to keep a low profile by not voicing her opinion regarding the ill-treatment of the women of Pakistan. I will say this: Ray helped both my son and me maintain our sanity when my wife seemingly disappeared off the face of the earth. She is a remarkable individual, sir, and you must feel blessed to have her as your wife."

"There are no words to express my love and respect for my wife. She is the most wonderful gift God has given me. I'm sure Sid has shared with you that we are having a child very soon, and I must return home by the first of June."

Simon's gaze held steady. "Blake, please listen to what I'm going to say to you: you must concentrate on your health. The most important thing you can do while you are here is to rest and be peaceful, and above all other things, get plenty of sleep. Sleep will help your system adjust to the infusions so the serum can do its work. You are going to get through all of this. I am here to help you each and every day. I believe you have a cell phone, so I can stay in communication with you and the 'healer' who administers your infusions, right?"

"Yes. Sid, would you give Simon the phone now?"

Sid handed it over. "Yes, it's simple to use, and there are instructions in the box. Let me know if you need any help with it."

Simon pocketed the phone. "Good. I'll be in contact tomorrow morning with the exact time of your first infusion. Blake, I won't let you down. Ray trusts me, and that means I will do everything in my power to see this through."

Blake met his eyes, his voice steady. "Then I will trust you too, Simon."

Simon placed a hand over his heart and nodded. "We'll not disappoint. Get some rest, my friend. I will see you tomorrow."

As the door closed behind Simon, Sid exhaled and turned to Blake. "Step one is in motion."

Blake leaned back into his chair, his eyes drifting once more to the view outside. "Yes. And now, all we can do is wait and believe."

Outside, the stars began to appear, one by one, over the peaks of Hunza Valley. A silent promise from heaven—hope was still alive.

Chapter Twenty-Eight

Ray floated effortlessly on her back, the gentle waves lapping against her skin as the sun warmed her face. Her rounded belly rose above the water, a visible reminder that life was about to change forever.

Two more weeks.

That was all that stood between her and holding the love of her life again. A week after that, she and Blake would be holding the greatest love of their lives—their child. Their miracle.

All thoughts were positive, even though some of Sid's communication regarding Blake gave her a few concerns. He looked thin. Too thin. His normally strong, commanding presence seemed dimmed. But when they spoke, he sounded like himself—steady, sure, unwavering. Was she imagining the concern in Sid's voice? She knew that, without a doubt, God Almighty would carry all of them through this ordeal.

Ray had taken the liberty of calling Rachel and explaining that her dad was in Pakistan taking some medical treatments, so if she did not hear from him, she would know why. Blake had blocked all callers from his phone other than Ray. This was at Simon's suggestion. Any negatives would slow down the healing process. Rachel had Ray's number if she decided to inquire about the welfare of her dad.

As Ray stepped out of the water onto the sand, she felt a sharp pain in her lower back. Ray froze, pressing a hand to her belly.

That was different.

She inhaled slowly, trying to steady herself, but as she took a few steps toward the cottage, the pain came again—sharper this time.

Journey, her loyal companion, was already waiting at the door, sensing something was off. He wagged his tail but stayed close, his brown eyes full of concern.

Ray reached for her phone.

"Hi there, fella. I gotta find my phone. We may have a baby on the way!"

Her fingers shook slightly as she dialed.

"Hey, Ray! What's up?" Rihards answered, his usual calm demeanor instantly putting her at ease.

"I may be going into labor."

A beat of silence. Then, his voice sharpened with urgency. "I'll be right there!"

Rihards was at her side in less than five minutes. "Okay, let's get you in the car and onto the hospital now."

"Thanks, sweetheart. I'm so glad I have you."

"I'm giving Aria a call, too. How are you doing with the pain?" Rihards asked.

"Okay, but it is intense."

"Aren't you going into labor a little early?"

"Probably three weeks earlier than I expected."

"Could it be a false alarm?"

"It could be Braxton Hicks, but I cannot be sure."

"Have you notified your doctor yet?"

"No. After you get me in the ER, take my phone and call my obstetrician; his name is listed in my contacts. Just drop me off and go park. I'll check in and see you in a minute."

As soon as they reached the hospital, Aria pulled up right behind them, practically sprinting out of the car.

"Are we having a baby today?" she asked, breathless.

"Don't know. It could be a false alarm."

"Okay. Let's go see what's happening."

When they checked with the ER desk, they were told that the ER doctor was with Ray and would give them an update as soon as he could.

Aria said, "Well, for Blake's sake, I hope this is not real labor."

The ER physician called for Mr. Giddings. Rihards stood up, approached the doctor, and asked, "Is she in labor?"

"No. I don't believe she is right now, but she is carrying the baby low, and sometimes, certain nerves can be affected and cause a great deal of back pain. Ray says she wants to go home. I suggested she just stay the night and go home in the morning if the pain subsides, but she insists she is fine and needs to get home for her dog, Journey."

That sounded exactly like Ray.

"We can spend the night at her place, and if anything develops, we'll bring her right in."

"Sorry, I did not introduce myself. I'm Dr. Whitley. Ray's obstetrician was unavailable, but I think he would concur with my findings. I think you have a fine idea to stay the night with her. We'll have her discharged and ready to go in about ten minutes."

Thanks, Dr. Whitley. I guess we could see you again later tonight, but we are hopeful that her baby will wait three more weeks so Ray's husband can be here. He is currently abroad."

"I think, if this was a false alarm, she would not deliver for three more weeks. This is just an educated guess, though."

"Sounds good. We'll see you in three weeks!" said Rihards. And they all knew it wouldn't be long now.

Chapter Twenty-Nine

Simon knocked on the door of Blake's suite. Sid walked quickly to let him in. Blake was finally getting some much-needed rest, and Sid had no intention of disturbing him.

"Come in, Simon." Sid shook his hand and smiled.

Simon asked, "How is our patient?"

"He had such a restless night, so I wanted him to sleep longer this morning."

"We have an assistant coming to administer the infusion this morning. As you know, this is the last one."

"Is this a reliable physician?" Sid asked.

"Very. She's been working on staff and administering these infusions for several years."

"Simon, I'm concerned about Blake's condition. He seems so weak and has lost quite a bit of weight."

"Sid, this is normal. He is on a diet that has been low in carbs, consisting mostly of vegetables with minimal fruits. The diet, alone, works to starve the cancer. As soon as he gets more carbs, his strength will come back in a few days, and of course, we'll be finished with the infusions, too. His body has been working hard to flush out all cancerous toxins, and naturally, he is in a weakened state. Trust me: in just two or three days, you'll see a huge difference," Simon explained.

There was another knock on the door. Simon opened it, welcomed Hannah in, and introduced her to Sid.

She asked, "Where shall I set up the equipment?"

Sid requested she give him a moment to awaken Blake and prepare him for the infusion.

"Good morning, Blake. Great news. We are ready to administer your last infusion. Are you ready?" Sid asked.

"I've been waiting for five weeks."

"I see you've not lost your sense of humor. Okay, buddy. Let's get this show on the road!"

Simon introduced Hannah to Blake. She smiled and gave him a wink. "We are giving you a small amount of vitamin B-12 in this infusion in hopes it will put a dance in your step so you can get back to Ray before your baby arrives!"

Blake's tired eyes lit up. "Oh, so you know Ray?"

"Most everyone in our community knows Ray. She is a celebrity here. She gave life to our existence in *National Geographic*. If it had not been for her talent and insight, our tourism would have withered on the vine," Hannah said.

Blake just smiled and softly said, "Ray rarely talks about herself. She is mostly just in the moment. I've never met anyone like her."

"Who knows? One day, the three of you may decide to make a trip over here."

Blake's gaze drifted toward the mountains visible through the window. "I'll never forget the beauty of this place, not only the majestic mountains and fertile valleys but the generosity and kindness of the people in this community. Thank you so much for helping me. I have the faith to believe I will be home to see our baby born."

Simon placed a steady hand on Blake's shoulder. "We believe in miracles here, Blake. And I have a feeling you'll be home in time to meet your child."

Blake nodded, closing his eyes briefly. "I believe that too."

Sid glanced at Simon, his eyes misting over.

They had come here hoping for a miracle.

And now, they were all expecting one.

Chapter Thirty

The morning air was crisp, carrying the scent of salt from the sea and freshly turned earth from the garden. Ray sat on the back patio, Journey sprawled beside her, his head resting on her lap. The baby stirred within her, a gentle reminder of the life about to enter the world. She couldn't believe how much had changed in such a short time.

Rihards and Saxton had gone above and beyond to move her into the new cottage, with Rihards purchasing dairy products and fresh fruit for them. He also gathered fresh vegetables and brought them to the new cottage. Aria had stocked the kitchen, Sid and Blake were on their way home, and now, everything was in place for their family to finally be together.

Ray never imagined she would be in their new place before the baby arrived. This also spun Rihards and Aria into action regarding setting a date to get married. Both were anticipating moving into Ray's original cottage.

Her peaceful thoughts were interrupted by the sharp ring of her phone. Journey lifted his head, ears perked. "Now, who could that be so early in the morning? Journey, I wish you could bring me my phone, boy!"

She managed to push herself to a standing position and slowly and carefully walked into the kitchen to grab her phone.

Out of breath, she managed a faint but audible "Hello."

"This is Rachel. May I speak to Ray?" she asked.

"This is she."

"I'm calling about my dad. I've been very concerned since I've not been able to contact him. Would you tell me what is going on, please?" Rachel asked.

"Rachel, there is quite a bit of information to share, and at this point, I do not presume to know all the answers. I'll try to simplify things for you, though. Your dad has been ill with lung cancer for some time. Only recently has he consented to accept treatments with the hope of extending his life or possibly being cured. He has been in Pakistan for five weeks and is due back in Cayman the day after tomorrow."

Silence.

Then, Rachel said flatly, "I cannot imagine why my dad has not told me any of this."

"Rachel, we would be happy to see you if you would like to come visit, and I'm sure your dad could share what is on his heart then," Ray said.

"Just have Dad call me when he gets in. I'm sorry to hear about his illness. Thank you for letting me know some of the details. Goodbye."

Ray listened to the click of the call ending and sighed deeply. Her heart ached for the brokenness between Blake and his daughter. She closed her eyes.

Dear Father, please soften Rachel's heart and help her reconnect with her dad. I know his heart must be aching because of their broken relationship. You, Father, can bring healing, restoration, and renewal; please let it be."

Journey suddenly jumped up and barked.

"What is it, boy?" Ray asked.

She walked to the front door and opened it.

"Blake!"

He stood there, looking thin but alive, his eyes filled with love. Before she could take another breath, she was in his arms. Tears streamed down both their faces as they clung to each other.

Sid, watching the reunion, felt his own throat tighten. The love between them was something rare—unshakable, unbreakable.

Finally, Sid stepped forward, guiding them both to the sofa. They continued holding each other, crying, laughing, breathing each other in.

Ray stroked Blake's cheek and asked, "How did you manage to get home so quickly? I was not expecting you for a couple of more days!"

"Sid changed our flight to an earlier one, and after the last infusion, I had a surge of energy and knew I could make it home early. I slept most of the time we were flying, and since the flights were so long, I'm rested and ready for you to have our child! Is your suitcase ready?"

Ray laughed and held him close again. "My suitcase has been packed since we had a false alarm two weeks ago. It was a dry run to the hospital with just Braxton Hicks contractions, so after that, I got serious about our baby's arrival. The baby will be here any time now!"

"Do you feel up to doing a slow walk-through of our new home?" Ray asked.

"I do, but only if you will make a pot of your bold and rich coffee for Sid and me."

"Sure thing. I'll also whip up a little breakfast for the three of us." Looking down at Journey, she added, "Four of us."

Sid and Blake walked through the cottage and out into the backyard. Blake could not believe so much had been accomplished during his absence.

"Oh, Sid, it is so good to be home! Ray is home. She would make any place a paradise, would she not?"

"Blake, she is full of love, courage, and faith. I've never met anyone like her. She is about to have a child, yet she is laboring in the kitchen to prepare a most excellent meal for us and is thrilled to do it!"

Blake's eyes shone with pride. "That's my wife!"

Ray called from the kitchen window, "Sid, would you come to help me carry trays outside?"

"Coming right away!" Sid said with enthusiasm. "I'll handle it all. Just make yourself comfortable and enjoy your new backyard!"

Blake looked toward the back fence and saw the beginnings of moonflower vines. It really was a magical plant. When it first starts to sprout leaves, they are angular in shape, but when it is ready to produce blossoms, the leaves change to a heart-like shape. Many mysteries unveil themselves in nature.

Ray asked, "Sweetheart, do you feel like eating?"

"I'll try a little. I still have no appetite, but I'll get it back with the wonderful meals you prepare."

The three of them enjoyed their breakfast together. Ray mentioned that Rachel had called earlier.

Blake said, "I will call her when I feel more like myself. I'm just too weak to even think at the moment."

Ray reached for his hand. "Whenever you're ready."

Ray asked Sid to clear the dishes from the patio while she escorted Blake to their bedroom.

"Lie down, sweetheart, and I will stay right by your side. Our faithful Journey is right beside your side of the bed. He missed you, too."

Blake felt her stomach and laid his head against the top of her stomach by her heart. "I want to hear two heartbeats."

"We want to hear your heartbeat, too. I missed you more than I could ever express."

Ray, Blake, and Journey stayed together and fell asleep. After enjoying the backyard and having quiet time, Sid cleaned the kitchen and gently shut the front door behind him.

He thought to himself, 'Mission accomplished, and what a mission it was!'

Chapter Thirty-One

It was a Friday on May 31st when Ray had been in labor for four hours. Blake had only been home for two days and barely regained his strength. Ray was so concerned that he was wearing himself out sitting with her while she was in labor, but he would not budge. The last time Ray's cervix was checked, she was almost crowning.

"Blake, sweetheart, you look so weary."

"You are not to concern yourself. I will be fine. I would not miss seeing our child come into the world for anything. Now, let's get you through this. You're doing amazing, sweetheart. Just a little longer."

Ray clung to his voice, his presence, as another wave of pain overtook her. She had endured hours of contractions, but this time, she cried out—a raw, unrestrained sound that cut straight through Blake's heart.

Seeing her in pain was unbearable. His body, still weak from treatment, protested as he pushed himself up from the chair. But he ignored it, rushing to the hallway.

"We have a baby coming!"

Two nurses came in and checked Ray. "Page the doctor; let's get her to the delivery room. Mr. Forsyth, please follow us. You two are about to have a baby!"

Blake took Ray's hand as they wheeled her down the corridor.

"I'm right here, Ray. We're so close."

She nodded through the pain, gripping his fingers tightly.

The doctor was suited up. "Hey Ray, remember me?"

"Oh, yes. You are Dr. Whitley, the ER doctor."

"Right. And this must be your husband."

Blake extended his hand. "Yes, I'm Blake. I just made it in time for the big event!"

Dr. Whitley nodded. "Perfect timing. Okay, folks. This is the grand event. Everything is fine."

As soon as Ray was settled on the delivery table, Blake went to her side and held her hand.

"Ray, give me one long, easy push. That's all we need, and your baby will arrive."

And then, the most beautiful sound filled the room.

A baby's cry. Strong. Certain. Alive.

Blake's breath hitched, and tears immediately blurred his vision.

Dr. Whitley said, "We have a good-sized baby boy. Mr. Forsyth, you have a son."

Ray gasped, then laughed through her tears. "A boy, Blake! We have a son!"

Blake could only nod, overwhelmed with emotion. The tiny, wailing bundle was carefully placed in Ray's arms.

"Look at him," Blake whispered, voice thick with awe. "He's so beautiful… and that hair! He's got a full head of it."

Ray, exhausted but radiant, simply smiled, drinking in every perfect detail of their son.

Dr. Whitley stepped closer. "Ray, would it be okay for Mr. Forsyth to hold him while we place a few sutures?"

She nodded, already knowing how much this moment would mean to Blake.

Blake hesitated as the nurse carefully transferred the tiny boy into his arms. He was so small, so delicate, yet so full of life.

A miracle.

Blake ran a gentle finger over his son's cheek, then pressed a soft kiss to his forehead. "Hey, little man. I'm your dad."

The weight of those words settled deep in his soul. He had made it—through the illness, the treatments, the doubts. He had fought to be here for this.

And now, here he was, holding his greatest reason to keep going.

"You can take him to meet his family while we finish up with Ray," the nurse suggested.

Blake hesitated. "Are you sure, sweetheart?"

Ray nodded. "Go. Introduce our son."

The waiting room was buzzing with nervous energy. Sid, Rihards, Aria, and Saxton sat in anticipation, hanging onto every sound beyond the closed doors.

Then, finally—

Blake stepped out, cradling the tiny bundle in his arms.

A collective breath of relief swept through the room.

Aria was the first to speak, pressing her hands to her heart. "Oh my goodness, he looks just like you, Blake!"

Rihards said, "I see a little red in that dark hair, maybe a little bit of Ray!"

Sid just smiled as tears fell from his eyes. He was happy, relieved, and grateful to God for having made this journey with all these remarkable people. They were indeed family.

Saxton was generally not outspoken, but he said, "I can't wait to teach him how to use a hammer to build his own treehouse!"

Everyone laughed and rejoiced over the miraculous event!

Chapter Thirty-Two

After everyone gave their opinions on a name, they decided on Byron Max Forsyth, or Max for short.

Little Max had been home just under a week when his half-sister visited for a surprise.

Blake managed to call Rachel two days after Max was born and explained all the details of their lives over the past few months. Rachel had been shocked to know about the gravity of her dad's illness but even more shocked that she had a baby brother.

But she had her own burdens. An investment gone wrong had left her in financial ruin. Though she was drowning in debt, pride kept her from admitting that she had defied her father's advice and failed spectacularly. Her mother had urged her to mend ties with Blake and seek help, but the thought of humbling herself made her stomach twist.

Ray was sitting in bed nursing Max, and the morning sunshine bathed the entire bedroom. She could not thank her heavenly Father enough for the little miracle she had in her arms nor for the fact that her loving husband was home, safe and sound.

Over the past week, she had watched Blake regain his strength, bit by bit, even filling out some of the weight he had lost. And this morning, he had outdone himself.

"For you, my beautiful wife."

She looked up to see him standing in the doorway, holding a breakfast tray. On it, a warm meal, a steaming cup of coffee, and a single rose in a delicate blue vase.

"Blake, you didn't need to go to this trouble. I could have put Max in his crib and come to the dining room."

"Nonsense," he said with a wink. "Give me Max, and I'll rock him while you enjoy breakfast in bed."

Ray smiled, but her eyes lingered on the small blue vase. "Blake, where did you find this exquisite blue vase?"

"Sid discovered it and ordered it. Actually, this is our celebration vase on behalf of Max. It is blue for our baby boy!"

Ray felt her heart swell. "What could be better than eating breakfast in bed with the two most wonderful treasures of my life right beside me? I'm overwhelmed."

A sudden knock at the front door interrupted their moment.

Blake and Ray exchanged a look. It was still early.

"Sweetheart, just place Max in his crib. Before you check on our visitor, shut the bedroom door while I finish the scrumptious breakfast you prepared for me."

"Just relax and enjoy," Blake said.

There was another knock on the door. Blake opened the door to find Rachel standing there, looking poised yet slightly uncertain.

"Hi, Dad! Surprise, it's me!" Rachel announced.

"Rachel, please come in. Is everything okay? This is such a surprise."

"Yes, Dad. Everything is fine," she said, though the tightness in her voice hinted otherwise.

"Come on in and have a seat here in the dining room. I'll pour you a cup of coffee and get you some breakfast," Blake graciously said.

She waved a dismissive hand. "Not necessary. I've already had room service at the hotel."

"Okay. Well, I'm going to serve myself a plate of sustenance here and get my energy level up!"

"Why isn't someone preparing breakfast for you?" Rachel asked.

"Because I am serving 'that someone' this morning, and that remark was quite unnecessary." His voice softened. "What's going on with you, Rachel?"

She exhaled, pressing her fingers against her temple. "I'm sorry, Dad. Please forgive me."

"Of course. Now, talk to me."

"Do you remember when I asked you to invest with me, and you declined?"

"Yes. I do."

"The investment went sour, and I lost all my savings and more. I've had to borrow money, and I'm not certain I can make my loan payments right now."

Blake inhaled sharply but remained composed. "Rachel, I have a trust fund set up for you. I had allocated all my assets, investments, and dividends to various trusts about two months ago before I left for treatment in Pakistan. I would be happy to arrange for you to draw monthly from this before my death. We'll allow the distribution to be the amount you need to pay off your loan. How does that sound?"

"Why can't I have the entire trust fund amount and make decisions regarding my business affairs accordingly?" Rachel asked with an edge to her voice.

Blake swallowed hard and paused before speaking. "I'll need some time to think about all of this, Rachel. In the meantime, I want you to meet Ray and Max and enjoy your visit with us."

Rachel glanced toward the hallway. "Dad, it's early. Why don't I go back to the hotel and come back this evening for introductions?"

"This evening? Why not come over for lunch?"

"I have business to handle. I'll drop back around five o'clock if that's okay with you and your wife."

"Of course. We'll look forward to your visit. Plan to have dinner with us and meet some of our friends, too."

Before exiting, she walked to the front door and said, "See you at five."

Blake thought: where has my lovely, affectionate daughter disappeared to?

The patio was a vision of warmth and comfort. A handcrafted wooden crib stood beneath the soft glow of string lights, a fluffy comforter cradling little Max. A cool breeze carried the scent of moonflowers, mingling with the rich aroma of the catered feast.

Sid and Rihards had surprised Ray that afternoon with a beautiful eight-person patio table, complete with a weather-proof tablecloth and a vase brimming with fresh flowers—a gift from Aria.

As the guests gathered, Blake marveled at how this eclectic group had become family over the past year. They had saved him and Ray in more ways than one.

Blake called Sid and asked him to secure a caterer for the evening event that morning. The only task Blake and Ray were responsible for was making beverages for dinner. Ray made freshly squeezed orange juice, and Blake made a gallon of tea.

When Rachel finally arrived, she seemed startled to see so many people.

Blake took her by the hand. "Let me introduce you to everyone, Rachel. Of course, you know my faithful friend from years ago," he said as he stopped in front of Sid.

Rachel extended her hand, "Sid, it is so good to see you again."

"And this is Rihards and his soon-to-be-wife, Aria. This gentleman is Saxton. And finally, this is my beautiful wife, Ray and your little brother, Max," Blake proudly announced.

Rachel blinked, momentarily speechless. "I... I wasn't expecting a dinner party."

"Rachel, all of the people present are our family. Everyone has helped in numerous ways to take care of Ray and me this past year. I would not have survived without their help and love, so get comfortable." Blake said.

Ray stood up and said, "Rihards, if you would say grace, we'll all sit down and enjoy this wonderful meal."

Throughout the meal, Rachel mostly listened and observed. From time to time, her gaze drifted toward Saxton.

His quiet presence intrigued her, and there was something about the way his hands moved—steady, deliberate, capable.

After the meal, music floated through the air. Blake pulled Ray into a dance, spinning her as if they were teenagers. Aria and Rihards followed.

Then, Saxton turned to Rachel.

"May I have this dance?" His voice was smooth, confident yet gentle.

Rachel hesitated before slipping her hand into his. His grip was warm—assured. As they swayed, she felt something unexpected: a sense of possibility.

Sid cradled Max and hummed softly to the music. Laughter, music, and the scent of moonflowers filled the night air.

And for the first time in a long time, Rachel felt something stir within her—a longing for belonging.

Chapter Thirty-Three

Over the course of Rachel's visit, her attitude slowly shifted—a complete one-eighty. She began to see the goodness in life through connections with Christians. At first, she had kept her walls up, uncertain and distant. But as the days passed, she began to see life through a different lens—one of faith, grace, and unexpected kindness.

Rihards took her to the gallery, sharing how he had become a part of Blake and Ray's lives. His story of redemption, loss, and purpose stirred something in her—a realization that she, too, could find a new beginning.

Aria invited her along to the local artisan shops, where she sold her handcrafted creations to eager tourists. Rachel admired the passion in her work, the way she poured love into each piece. It made her wonder—when was the last time she had created something with joy, rather than desperation?

Sid, ever the steady presence, took her for an evening walk along the beach, recounting the details of his journey to Pakistan with her father. As he spoke, she felt an ache in her chest—how much had she missed by staying away?

Most surprising of all was Saxton. He had taken an interest in her, and to everyone's astonishment, Rachel seemed just as taken with him. He took her snorkeling, his patience evident as he guided her through the gentle waters. When he suggested she learn to scuba dive, she had laughed, playfully swatting his arm.

"Not this time," she had said with a teasing smirk. "Next visit."

She meant it.

Day was breaking and the world was not yet stirring. Ray yawned and quietly slipped out of bed. She nursed Max, nestled him into Blake's waiting arms, and stepped out onto the beach, breathing in the crisp salty air.

It was time. Time to return to her routine—morning walks, exercise, and quiet moments of meditation with her Lord.

The horizon stretched before her in a masterpiece of colors. The first rays of sunlight kissed the sky, chasing away the fading moon and the last of the stars. The waves rolled in rhythmic symphonies, whispering praises to the Creator who had set them in motion.

She closed her eyes, inhaling deeply.

Dear Father, You have blessed me beyond what I could have ever imagined.

Her heart swelled as she thought of her husband—the man who had been chosen for her. She thought of Byron, the love she had lost, and how God had stitched together the torn fabric of her soul through Byron's brother, Rihards.

She thought of Max, the precious miracle she never thought she'd hold, and how through him, God had given her a second chance at the beauty of motherhood.

Your gifts are humbling, Lord. I thank You with all my heart.

A gentle breeze stirred her hair as she whispered her next request.

Father, give Blake the courage to trust in Your control over his life. Be merciful and grant us good results from his chest scan this afternoon. Let us rest in the peace that only You can provide. In the Holy Name of Jesus, Amen.

A soft rustling behind her made her smile. She didn't have to turn around to know who had found her.

Journey.

The loyal dog trotted to her side, nuzzling her hand as if sensing the weight of her thoughts.

"Oh, Journey," she murmured, stroking his head. "What a glorious day, don't you think, boy?"

The ocean's foam crackled along the shore, greeting the day with its own melody.

"You've been with me through it all. A true sign of God's providence."

She quickened her pace, walking another half-mile before turning back toward home.

Home.

What a powerful word. It wasn't just a structure. It was bonds, love, comfort, and trust. Matters of the heart.

As she neared their house, her heart swelled with anticipation.

There, standing in front of their home, was Blake.

He held Max securely in his arms, gazing out toward the vast stretch of ocean. Though he didn't speak, she could sense his thoughts—the quiet, weighty contemplation of what the day would bring.

Ray paused, pressing a hand over her heart.

God, please give him Your confidence. Let him feel Your peace.

Then, with renewed strength, she walked forward—toward the love waiting for her.

Chapter Thirty-Four

The island buzzed with the arrival of tourists, their eager footsteps filling the streets, their laughter carried on the ocean breeze. It was the height of the season, and Rihards worked late into the night, his hands tirelessly bringing life to the canvases, ensuring the gallery remained filled with fresh pieces.

Ray, too, had found inspiration. She had begun capturing the faces of the islanders—her family, her friends, the people who had become part of her heart. Each photograph told a story, a glimpse into the love and resilience that surrounded her.

She knew exactly who she wanted to help complete these works of art.

When she approached Saxton about crafting unique frames, his face lit up.

"I've been waiting for you to ask," he said with a grin.

With meticulous care, he secured quality rosewood for Ray's photographs, its deep hues complementing the warmth of each image. For Rihards' paintings, he chose rich-figured walnut, its intricate grains enhancing the depth of his artistry. Each frame, handcrafted with purpose, was more than an accessory—it was part of the story.

Meanwhile, Blake had been strategic, placing carefully curated ads in renowned art magazines. The gallery had gained a reputation, and with another exhibit planned for March, excitement was building.

But amidst the art and ambition, love was in the air.

Aria had sold her cottage.

She and Rihards had chosen a date—Valentine's Day. The simplicity of it suited them. They didn't long for extravagant honeymoons or distant destinations. Instead, they desired Ray's old cottage, where their love had blossomed.

Aria had already begun weaving her touch into the home, carefully adding small details that made it their own. Yet, she and Rihards remained faithful to their evening tradition—walking the beach together, stopping by the cottage to feed the koi before picking fresh fruit and vegetables from the garden. Their love was quiet but deeply rooted, just like the life they were building.

Not all departures were joyful.

Sid had returned to Scotland, but this time, leaving had been harder. His heart had grown deeply attached to little Max, and the bond he shared with Rihards was unshakable. To Sid, he was like a son.

Before he left, Blake received his scan results.

They weren't what everyone had prayed for, but at least the tumors had not grown. The news was neither entirely hopeful nor devastating—it was somewhere in between. A space where faith was tested, yet unbroken.

Sid watched his friends carefully in the days that followed, searching for signs of sorrow or fear. But Blake and Ray, ever steadfast, pressed forward, their joy undiminished. They walked in peace, in the quiet assurance that God was in control.

The night before Sid's departure, Ray visited him at the villa. They spoke for hours—of faith, of trust, of the unshakable foundation that carried them through each trial.

She shared with him the passage that had anchored her and Blake the night before his scan results:

"Those who are righteous will be long remembered. They do not fear bad news; they confidently trust the Lord to care for them. They are confident and fearless and can face their foes triumphantly."
—Psalm 112

Sid had listened, a deep warmth filling his chest. He had always known Blake and Ray to be resilient, but now, he understood the source of their strength.

On his flight back to Scotland, a thought settled heavily on him—one he could not ignore.

It was time.

Perhaps it was Blake's prognosis, or perhaps it was something deeper—a quiet knowing within him. But as the plane carried him home, Sid resolved to put his affairs in order.

He would contact his attorney. Write his will.

Not out of fear, but out of faith. Because he knew.

No matter when his final breath came, his soul had always belonged to God. And when the moment arrived, he would simply be returning home.

Two weeks after Sid's departure, the phone rang.

Blake answered, his heart sinking the moment he heard the voice on the other end.

Sid had passed away.

A heart attack in the quiet of the night. Swift. Unexpected.

And yet… not entirely.

Blake swallowed hard as the caller relayed Sid's final wishes.

He wished to be cremated and for his ashes to be scattered in the ocean near the cottages and villas in Cayman.

Near them.

Near the people he had loved.

He had left all his assets to Rihards.

Blake closed his eyes, emotion swelling in his chest. Sid had known.

Somehow, he had known. And he had made sure to leave behind a final act of love.

Blake stepped outside, gazing toward the ocean, where the waves kissed the shore with quiet reverence. The breeze carried the scent of salt and memories.

"Rest easy, my friend," he whispered. "You are home."

Chapter Thirty-Five

With just a few days before the wedding and a month until the next gallery exhibition, Rihards poured himself into his work, moving from one canvas to the next as if his very soul were spilling onto them. He had never painted so much in such a short time. It was as if joy and grief had collided within him, manifesting through his art.

He toiled day and night, running on little sleep.

The loss of Sid had been a crushing blow. Grief clung to him like a heavy cloak, and though he knew God would carry him through, the pain remained raw. Losing Sid so soon after his mother's passing made the weight of absence almost unbearable.

But through it all, Rihards kept his eyes on those who had endured much and still walked forward. Ray and Blake. They

Where Moonflowers Dance

lived with a quiet, unwavering faith—not defined by the visible, but by the invisible.

Somewhere in the early hours of morning, exhaustion overtook him, and he collapsed onto the sofa. The next thing he knew, a soft tapping at the sliding glass door stirred him awake.

Blinking, he turned his head.

Ray stood outside, smiling.

She looked fresh, expectant—ready to embrace the day.

Rihards groaned as he sat up, rubbing the sleep from his eyes before pushing himself to his feet. With slow steps, he crossed the room and slid the door open.

"Ray?" His voice was groggy. "Is everything okay?"

"Of course. But I haven't seen you in days. I was a little concerned. Are you okay?"

He exhaled, running a hand through his disheveled hair. "I may not be right now... but I will be. Sid's death hit me harder than I expected. I miss him terribly. Maybe it's because it came so soon after losing my mom."

Ray nodded knowingly. "This too will pass, Rihards."

He managed a weak smile. "Tea?"

"I'd love a cup."

As he moved to the kitchen, he asked, "How are Blake and Max?"

Ray's face softened. "Both are sleeping like babies. I left Max curled up in Blake's arms. He already favors his dad so much. It makes me smile every time I see them together. I've never witnessed such love and devotion from a father as Blake has for Max."

Rihards nodded. "Sid was like that for me."

His voice faltered, and he set down the teacups. "He was the quiet presence in my life, always giving, never asking for anything in return. We talked about everything... and sometimes, we didn't have to talk at all. The silence was enough."

His shoulders trembled, and before he could stop himself, the tears came.

Ray moved beside him, draping a gentle arm over his shoulders.

"A good cry is cleansing for the soul," she whispered. "When Byron died, I bottled everything up. I refused to acknowledge my grief. It nearly broke me. But God hears every cry, Rihards. He will carry you through this, just as He carried me.

She hesitated, then continued softly.

"I loved your brother with every fiber of my being. Losing him left a hollow space in my soul. For years, I felt like I was missing a part of myself. But... Blake and Max, and even you, Rihards, have helped heal that void."

Rihards took a shaky breath, nodding. "That's... a beautiful way to put it. Thank you for sharing that with me."

After a moment, Ray glanced toward the hallway. "Can I see what you've been working on?"

Without hesitation, Rihards led her to the small guest bedroom.

When he opened the door, Ray's breath caught in her throat.

The walls were covered in scenes of the beach, candid portraits of strangers—but what stunned her most were the paintings of Max.

Her heart squeezed as she took in one piece in particular—Sid cradling Max, just a week after he was born.

Her fingers trembled as she reached out, almost as if she could touch the memory woven into the canvas.

"Rihards..." Her voice wavered. "These are incredible. Every single one of them. Your soul speaks through the eyes of the people you paint."

He let out a weary sigh. "I think grief finds its way out differently for everyone. Mine just happens to come out on canvas. And there's still so much inside of me that I need to paint. I suppose that's why I can't sleep anymore."

Ray turned to him and took his hand. "Come back to the living room with me. Let's talk a little longer."

As they settled onto the sofa, Rihards sighed heavily.

"There's something I need to confess," he admitted. "I feel like I've neglected Aria this past week. She's been handling so many wedding details—the minister, the flowers, my tux, her dress. She's so excited to be my wife, and I've been... lost in my grief. I hate that I've let my sorrow overshadow her joy."

Ray squeezed his hand. "Rihards, let's pray."

She closed her eyes, her voice steady and full of warmth.

"Father in Heaven, thank You for the emotions You've given us, for making us wonderfully complex. You've designed us to feel both joy and sorrow, but Lord, I ask that You help Rihards shift his focus now— to embrace the love and excitement You have placed before him. Aria is Your gift to him. Let him cherish her in this moment, to be honest and open with her, and to celebrate the life they are about to build together. In Jesus' Name, Amen."

When she opened her eyes, Rihards whispered, "Thank you, Ray. That means more than I can say."

Ray stood, stretching. "I should get going. But before I leave, promise me one thing?"

He lifted an eyebrow. "What's that?"

"Take a break from painting. Go for a run on the beach. And most importantly, surprise Aria. She's been working hard to turn my old cottage into your new home. I've seen it—Rihards, it's beautiful. And she did it all for you."

A slow smile spread across his face. "I'll change clothes and be off in fifteen."

Ray grinned, pulling him into a quick hug before heading toward the door. "Good. Now go remind your future wife why she fell in love with you."

As she walked away, Rihards felt something shift.

The weight of grief was still there, but it no longer consumed him.

He still had love. He still had life. And he would not let this moment pass him by.

Chapter Thirty-Six

Rachel had thought of nothing but returning to Cayman since she had arrived back in the States. She couldn't quite put her finger on it, but something deep inside her longed for the island in a way she had never longed for anything before. It was as if layers of her old self were being stripped away, piece by piece.

When she returned home, she made a point to start reading the Bible her dad had given her before she boarded her flight. Each day, she found herself growing more restless and disinterested in her career. In the last several days, she had spent hours reflecting on the lives of her family and the dear friends she had left behind in Cayman. Subtle changes were happening within her, things she couldn't quite explain.

She had started talking to God. At first, it was hesitant, uncertain. But now, she realized she was talking to Him all day.

God, have I found You, or have You found me?

Her fingers ran over the light blue leather cover of the Bible, its smooth surface comforting beneath her touch. A thought settled deep within her soul.

I'm being transformed. God, You've been here all along, and I've just now come home.

She reached for her phone and powered it on.

Today is the day to start a new journey.

She dialed her mother's number.

"Rachel, it's nice to hear from you," her mother greeted. "How are things going with your finances?"

Rachel took a steady breath. "Mom, I really can't say. I'm not interested in pursuing a career in finance anymore. That's actually why I called. I wanted to let you know—I'm moving to Cayman."

There was a beat of silence. "What?"

"I know this comes as a surprise, but I'm packing up my things and putting the rest in storage. My lease is up for renewal in a month, and I won't be signing again."

Her mother's voice tightened. "You're just going to abandon your career? Your clients? All the time and effort you've put in?"

"That's right," Rachel said firmly. "Since visiting Dad and getting to know the people in his life, I can see so clearly now. If I stay here, I'll just be chasing a superficial life—one that doesn't fulfill me."

Her mother let out a frustrated sigh. "You've worked so hard to build this career. I can't believe you'd just throw it all away."

Rachel closed her eyes for a moment. "It's not me anymore, Mom. My heart isn't in it. For the first time, I feel like I'm truly seeing what's real and what's worth my time."

"I think you need to give this more time. You're making a mistake."

"I know you're worried about me, but I promise, I'm going to be fine. Actually, I already am." She softened her tone. "I just wanted to let you know what's happening. I'll visit you soon, I promise."

Ending the call, she immediately dialed her dad.

"Dad, are you ready for this news?"

Blake's voice was calm. "What's on your mind, Rachel?"

"I'm coming back to Cayman—to stay."

A slow smile spread across his face. He turned toward Ray, covering the phone with his hand as he whispered, "Rachel is coming back."

Ray's eyes lit up, and she wrapped her arms around him. "An answer to my prayers."

Chapter Thirty-Seven

The grand day had finally arrived—Rihards and Aria would become husband and wife. Their wedding ceremony was set to take place in Aria's little church, a place that had been part of her life since childhood. Her parents had attended the church since they were young, and Aria had never known another home of worship. It was a close-knit fellowship where everyone knew one another, and love and support were abundant.

Aria's mother had plenty of help from the women in the congregation. The church's florist, a dear friend of the family, carefully arranged all the flowers to Aria's specifications. The priest, who had known Aria since she was a child, had taken a personal interest in counseling both her and Rihards, preparing them for their lifelong commitment to each other and to God.

Though Aria had no siblings, she cherished Ray like the sister she never had. In a gesture of deep affection, she asked Ray if she could wear her wedding dress rather than designing a new one. It was Aria's way of making Ray feel like family—something Ray and Blake had already done in more ways than one. They had sold their old cottage to Aria for a fraction of its market value, an act of kindness that humbled her. She adored them both, and Rihards felt the same way, especially toward Ray, to whom he was deeply devoted.

Rachel arrived just in time to attend the wedding alongside Blake and Ray. The small church was filled to capacity, with standing room only. Aria had asked Ray to sing *Our Father Who Art in Heaven* while Saxton played his guitar and Aria's mother accompanied on the piano. The three of them had practiced only once, but Aria insisted it had been perfect. Ray had not sung in front of an audience since her school days, but Aria had overheard her singing in the garden weeks earlier and couldn't resist asking her. At first, Ray had hesitated, but with some gentle persuasion, she had agreed.

The ceremony began. From the loft above the sanctuary, Ray stood at the railing, ready to sing. As the music started, all eyes turned toward the aisle. Aria, radiant and graceful, walked arm in arm with her father toward the altar, where Rihards stood beaming beside the priest. Ray's voice filled the space—soft, clear, and angelic. It was a moment of pure beauty, and when Aria's father kissed her cheek and placed her hand in Rihards', there was not a dry eye in the church.

The reception, arranged by the dedicated women of the congregation, was a joyous celebration. Every guest was invited to share in the couple's happiness. Laughter and love filled the air as friends and family gathered to bless the newlyweds. After an hour or so, Rihards took Aria's hand. With warm smiles and heartfelt goodbyes, they slipped away, eager to begin their new life together.

Instead of traveling far for a honeymoon, they chose to spend their first night as husband and wife in the very place where Ray and Blake had once begun their journey. But before Rihards carried Aria across the threshold of their cottage, they took a slow walk along the beach, watching the sun dip below the horizon.

As they walked hand in hand, Rihards turned to Aria, his voice full of wonder. "Aria, I'm happier than I've ever been. I never imagined my life could feel this complete, this blessed by God. Sometimes, I wonder if I'm dreaming."

Aria squeezed his hand, her heart full. "I feel the same way. When I met Ray and Blake, it set my feet on a different path—one that keeps surprising me every day. And you, Rihards, were the answer to my prayers. For as long as I can remember, I asked God to choose a husband for me, someone to walk this earthly journey with. Look how far and wide He searched to find me such a man. You are a good man, Rihards Giddings, and I love you with all my heart."

Chapter Thirty-Eight

Rachel had settled into a comforting morning routine with Saxton before he started his workday. Each morning, she would walk from the villa to his house, where he always had breakfast ready for them. After their meal, they would take a long walk along the beach, their conversations flowing as naturally as the waves beside them.

It was becoming increasingly clear to Rachel that what she felt for Saxton was far deeper than infatuation. There was something about him—his quiet confidence, his unwavering integrity—that reminded her of her dad. He never sought attention or recognition, but when he spoke, his words carried weight. His strength of character, quick wit, and warm smile made her admire him even more.

Since coming to Cayman, Rachel had learned so much about what truly mattered in life. The people she had met through her father had shown her a different way of living—one that was rich in purpose and connection. Her father had changed, too. Since meeting Ray, he had softened, viewing life in a way she had never seen before. While he had always been a wonderful father, his work had kept him distant. They had spent time together during her college years, but their conversations had always revolved around career ambitions rather than personal matters.

Ray was one of the most genuine people Rachel had ever met. In many ways, she reminded Rachel of Sid—kind, strong, and deeply grounded. It was no wonder her father had been drawn to her, just as he had been to Sid, his closest friend.

Saxton had never spoken to Rachel about a future together, but she knew, without hesitation, that she wanted to move forward with him. One night, when he had walked her back to the villa, he had kissed her. She had invited him to stay for a while, but he had declined. She suspected he might have been embarrassed by her forwardness. Aria had once mentioned that as far as she knew, Saxton had never been in a relationship. He had always been focused on his craft, taking great pride in his work. He was deeply respected by those who worked for him, as they knew they could rely on him to provide not just employment but stability for their families.

Reflecting on her first visit to Cayman, Rachel felt ashamed of the arrogance she had once carried. She had been blinded by her own desires, dismissing her father's feelings for Ray and the meaningful relationships he had built.

Lord, forgive me for the way I dismissed my father's happiness and all the people who have now become so dear to me. I was so consumed with my own selfish goals that I couldn't see what truly mattered. How did Saxton even see anything of worth in me back then? Thank You for taking my heart of stone and softening it with Your mercy and grace.

Please give me the opportunity to ask my father's forgiveness, too. Thank You, sweet Jesus.

Glancing at the time, Rachel realized she was already fifteen minutes late for breakfast. She grabbed her phone and quickly sent a text:

"Running a little late. See you soon."

Chapter Thirty-Nine

It had been a long day for Saxton. His breakfast with Rachel had started later than planned, and work had fallen behind schedule. By the time he got home, the sun was already beginning to set.

He sat down at the kitchen table with a cup of hot cocoa, the tiny marshmallows melting into the warmth of the drink. He had always liked something warm in the evenings—it took him back to winter holidays spent with his parents and sister. Every year, they gathered for Christmas at a ski resort, usually in Colorado or Utah. He could still picture the massive fireplaces in the lodges, the way he and his family would make new friends each season, singing carols and drinking hot cocoa by the fire.

The last Christmas they had planned together, he arrived at the resort a day early to hit the black slopes. His parents and sister preferred the intermediate runs and were supposed to meet him the next day. He had been waiting in the lodge, excited to see them, watching the entrance as time passed. They were late—two hours late. His phone rang, an unknown number. He answered, and in that moment, his world shattered. There had been a car accident between Denver and Breckenridge. His parents and sister had all died on impact.

He had endured the unimaginable, handling the details of a funeral for his entire family alone, selling his parents' home, settling their estate. He never finished his last semester of college. Instead, after making a few investments, he packed up and left, landing in Grand Cayman. The physical work of carpentry gave him something to focus on, something to quiet his grief. Woodworking had always been a passion of his, and slowly, he built a new life for himself. Cayman was nothing like home—no cold weather, no fireplaces, no painful reminders. The only piece of his past he held onto was the ritual of drinking hot chocolate.

Now, his thoughts were filled with Rachel. He had never had a serious relationship before, but watching Ray and Blake had shown him the kind of love he wanted. Ray had helped him understand the kind of woman he should wait for, and Blake had taught him how to treat someone he loved.

When he first met Rachel, he had been struck by her beauty. Her thick black hair, her striking blue eyes—eyes that seemed to hold something unspoken, a silent plea for help. From the moment he saw her, he had been drawn to her. He had known the image she projected wasn't who she truly was. There was something beneath it, something real, something worth knowing.

That was history now. He was completely in love with her.

Tonight was the night. He took a quick shower, dressed in shorts and a T-shirt, slipped on his running shoes, and bolted out the door, heading straight for the villa.

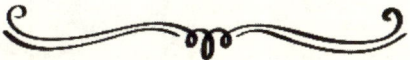

Rachel sat on the balcony, her thoughts filled with all the things she wanted to say to her dad. She wanted him to know how much she loved and admired him, how much she appreciated Ray's kindness, and how both of them had helped her grow in her faith.

The ocean stretched endlessly before her, the last remnants of the sunset reflecting off the water. She loved this time of day, loved watching God paint the sky with colors no human hand could recreate. Each sunset was unique, a masterpiece only the heart could truly comprehend.

From the corner of her eye, she saw Saxton running toward the villa. Her heartbeat quickened. He waved, and she motioned for him to come up.

When she answered the door, she gave him a soft hug and welcomed him in. "Would you like to sit out on the balcony and enjoy a cup of herbal tea with me?"

"Yes, I would like that very much."

"How was your day? I know I probably delayed you somewhat, and I apologize," she said softly.

"It's okay. There's no need to apologize. I look forward to being with you first thing in the morning."

They walked out onto the balcony and took their seats. The sky had dimmed to a deep blue, and the rhythmic sound of the waves provided a soothing backdrop to their conversation.

"I have a question to ask you, Rachel."

She turned to him, curious. "What's on your mind, Saxton?"

"At this point in our relationship, I'm not quite sure about your feelings for me, but I wanted to tell you that I am very much in love with you and would like for you to be my wife."

There was a brief pause before Rachel smiled. "Saxton, you rarely say anything unless it's worthy of being heard. You do get right to the point, don't you?"

"Yes. I've never seen the point of dancing around something that needs to be said."

Rachel took a deep breath, her heart full. "I do love you and want to spend the rest of my life with you."

Saxton stood, gently pulling her into his arms. "We will have a good life together, I promise."

He kissed her deeply, then pulled back just enough to look into her beautiful blue eyes before kissing her again.

Chapter Forty

Blake pulled Ray close, his fingers gliding through her long, silky hair. "I love the mornings with you," he murmured. "When the sunlight wakes us up, reminding us of all of God's goodness."

Ray smiled, pressing closer. "Darling, I have an idea. Let's ask Aria to stay with Max while we go snorkeling this morning."

"Perfect," Blake said, a playful glint in his eyes. "But for now, I have a better idea."

Aria heard her phone ringing and rushed to find it. "Hello!"

"Hey, Aria! You sound out of breath."

"Not really, just couldn't find my phone. How are you this fine morning?"

"We're well—feeling somewhat energetic. Would you be up for watching Max for a couple of hours while we go snorkeling?"

"Of course! My pleasure."

"Would an hour from now work?"

"Absolutely. I'll see you soon."

Ray called out to Blake, excitement in her voice. "Get your swimsuit on! Aria will take care of Max."

As she stepped into the bedroom, she giggled softly, watching Blake cradle their baby. "You know, this is as good as it gets—seeing you holding our son first thing in the morning. Watching the two of you share such pure, unconditional love." Her voice softened. "Oh, Blake, God has been so good to us. I pray we live a long life together, watching Max grow into a fine man like his dad."

Blake looked up, his expression full of devotion. "Sweetheart, you've taught me to live in the moment, to stay grounded in the eternal. And I rather enjoy it. Let's leave the past as memories and not worry about tomorrow or next week. Let's just hold tightly to the moments God has graced us with."

A knock on the door interrupted them.

"I think that's Aria," Ray said, grinning. "She's early! Get your swimsuit on, and let's enjoy this gorgeous morning!"

Ray opened the door and greeted Aria with a bright smile. "Are you ready for some of Max's sweet snuggles?"

"Can't wait! This is the first time you've let him out of your sight."

Ray laughed. "Not true! I've left him in his dad's arms a few times."

Aria shook her head with a knowing smile. "Ray, you take such good care of all your boys—Blake, Max, Journey, and Rihards. What would they do without you?"

"They are all so needed and loved," Ray said warmly. "But tell me, how are you and Rihards? Still in the honeymoon phase, I'd guess."

"Yes, Ray. How long does the honeymoon last?"

"Forever!" Ray declared.

Blake entered the kitchen, a towel slung over his shoulder. "I'm ready." He smiled at Aria. "Good morning! How are you and Rihards doing this week?"

"We couldn't be better. And we're all set for the next art showing at your gallery!"

"That's wonderful news. Just a few more weeks, and we'll have Rihards well on his way to being a sought-after artist."

Ray grabbed the duffle bag and snorkel masks. "Aria, enjoy our boy. We'll see you in a couple of hours."

Aria rocked Max gently. "Don't worry, I'll spoil him the whole time you're away."

Blake grinned. "By all means, spoil our boy."

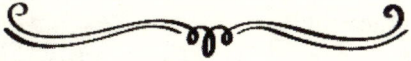

"Blake, let's hold our breath and dive to the ocean floor where the yellow and blue fish get up close and personal!"

Both dove, gliding through the cool water, running their hands over the soft sand, marveling at the sea life.

Blake spotted a small piece of brain coral shaped like a heart. When they surfaced, he placed it in Ray's palm.

Ray gasped. "What an unusual piece of coral! It's a real treasure."

Blake smiled. "I'm going to take another look below."

"Okay. I'll be right back after I put our little coral heart in the duffle bag."

Taking a deep breath, Blake swam down again, pushing toward the ocean floor. But suddenly, a powerful undercurrent gripped him. He knew not to fight it. He tried to swim parallel to the shore, but exhaustion crept in. The current pulled him farther out until, at last, it let go.

He broke the surface, gasping, looking toward the shore. Ray stood there, frantically waving, her hands motioning for him to move to the side of the current.

He tried. He swam. He floated. But his strength was gone. He knew.

A flood of images filled his mind—Ray's laughter, the touch of her hand, her wisdom and devotion, the way Max's tiny head smelled of innocence and love. Journey's warm snuggles.

Oh, God, he prayed silently. *I suppose it's time for me to come Home. Help Rihards to be a father to Max. Help my beautiful wife accept this, knowing I am at peace in Your arms.*

He lifted his hand in one final wave.

Ray watched, her heart pounding. *He sees me.*

But then—nothing.

Minutes passed. Frantic searching. Desperate prayers.

And then, an eerie stillness settled over her.

She knew.

He was gone.

Her body turned to stone. Her mind felt like shattered glass. And then, when she thought of the future, terror struck with a vengeance.

Oh, God. I know this is Your will, or You wouldn't have allowed it, but this pain—this agony—is breaking me apart. Help me, Jesus. Hold me together.

She wept, her sobs lost to the wind and waves.

The morning had passed. The sun had climbed higher. She had to go home.

Her body felt like it weighed a thousand pounds, but she forced herself forward. Max was waiting.

When Ray entered the front door, Aria sat in the living room, rocking Max in her arms.

Ray's steps faltered. The moment Aria looked up, she knew.

Ray reached out, taking Max, holding him as if she could shield him from what she had lost.

Her voice was barely a whisper.

"Blake is gone."

Chapter Forty-One

Ray and Pastor Lovell had carefully planned every detail of Blake's memorial service, scheduled for two weeks after he drowned. His body had yet to be found, and truthfully, Ray hoped it remained that way. She had first seen him on the beach, and the last time she saw him was there as well. One day, he appeared; one day, he disappeared. God had brought him into her life, and God had taken him away. The only thing keeping her sane was the certainty that she would see him again.

Aria and Rihards had stayed with Ray and Max since the accident, never leaving her side. When she cried, they cried. Max was their sunshine in the darkness, their daily reminder of Blake's love. Even Journey grieved—whining constantly for the first couple of days, sensing the loss as only a devoted dog could. He knew.

Because Blake was well-known in the community, the church was packed for his memorial service. Several people had asked Ray if they could say a few words about him during the service, and of course, she had agreed. She was grateful for their kindness, for their memories of the man she loved. Even the town mayor had asked to speak, a testament to Blake's impact on the lives around him.

After the service, the congregation gathered in the fellowship hall, where a beautifully prepared meal awaited. The church members had arranged everything, and Ray was humbled by the outpouring of love and support.

Rihards noticed how exhausted she was and knew she needed to go home. He quietly signaled Aria to take Max from her arms, then gently guided Ray toward the car. They bid their farewells and made their way home.

As they pulled into the driveway, they noticed a car already parked there. It was Saxton's. Rachel sat beside him, waiting for them to arrive.

Ray was the first to step out. Leaving Max in Aria's arms, she approached them with open arms.

"I'm so glad the two of you came tonight." She turned to Rachel, her voice full of warmth. "I've wanted to visit with you, to comfort you, but I haven't had the presence of mind to do so. Please, both of you, come in."

Inside, Rihards took it upon himself to prepare tea. He carried out two trays of steaming mugs along with a plate of blueberry scones he had warmed from the freezer. They all settled on the patio, where the night air carried a faint, comforting breeze.

Ray sat beside Rachel, wrapping an arm around her shoulders. Rachel wept, her sorrow pouring out in waves.

"I'm so sorry," she whispered over and over. "I never got the chance to tell my dad how I felt."

Tears streamed down her face as she looked at Ray.

"I was waiting for the perfect moment," she confessed. "I wanted to tell him how much I respected him. How much I respected his decision to marry you. But most of all, I wanted him to know how much I learned about love—real love—just by watching him with you and Max. It was love in its purest form."

Her voice broke, but she continued.

"I'll never forget Sid, either. Dad's faithful friend. He was blessed to witness the love you and Dad shared. Ray, we all were. You both made such a difference in our lives."

Ray wiped away a tear and squeezed Rachel's hand.

"I'm thankful God allowed others to see the divine love He placed in our hearts for each other." She took a deep breath. "Your dad was the first man I was ever with—first, last, and only."

Silence settled over them, heavy yet peaceful. Then, as if on cue, Max let out a sudden, joyful laugh.

Everyone turned to look.

Journey had placed his muzzle gently against Max's tiny hand, and Max erupted into another giggle, his eyes bright with delight.

Ray smiled, her heart swelling.

"God always gives us the ability to receive joy when we trust Him," she said softly.

A quiet moment passed before Saxton cleared his throat. His voice, usually reserved, was steady and full of purpose.

"I have something I'd like to share with everyone." He glanced at Rachel before continuing. "I believe now is the right time because we all need a new journey. Perhaps we can focus on what we have, rather than what we've lost."

All eyes turned to him.

Rachel reached for Ray's hand, her grip gentle but firm.

Saxton straightened his shoulders, speaking with a confidence rarely seen in him.

"I've asked Rachel to be my wife," he announced. "And she has accepted."

A wave of emotion rippled through the group.

Ray's face broke into a smile as she pulled Rachel into a warm embrace.

"This is glorious news," she said, her voice filled with genuine happiness. "I congratulate both of you."

Chapter Forty-Two

Ray had started taking Max to the beach when she walked Journey in the mornings after her cup of coffee. At only two, he was sure-footed and excited each and every morning to embark upon their journey. It was as though he were as addicted to their walks as Ray was to her first cup of coffee!

He had begun to lose some of his baby fat, his face taking on the strong features of his father. With every passing day, he looked more and more like Blake. She never tired of hearing people tell her how much Max resembled his dad—it was a bittersweet reminder, a gift wrapped in longing.

That morning, she encouraged Max to run and splash at the water's edge. He laughed with delight, falling a few times, but each time, he brushed the sand off his little swim trunks and stood right back up.

"Max, tell me what you see far out in the ocean," Ray asked, crouching beside him.

Max furrowed his brow, his little face full of concentration. "Water. Sky. Clouds."

His pronunciation was so clear it made her smile.

"And do you see anything else?" she prompted.

Max looked out at the horizon again, his dark eyes scanning the distance. Then he said, simply, "Man."

Ray's heart skipped. "Man?"

Max nodded.

"What does the man look like? Is he in the clouds?"

There was a long pause before Max answered. "Walks on water."

Ray's breath caught in her throat. "Max, come to me."

She scooped him up and held him close, sinking down onto the sand. His little head, full of dark curls, rested on her chest. She inhaled deeply, taking in his scent, the warmth of his small body pressed against hers.

Had her son seen something beyond what her own eyes could perceive? Was it a vision of Christ? Or had he seen Blake's spirit?

The thought made her tears come freely. She did not sob; she simply let them fall.

Max lifted his head, looking up at her with wide eyes. "Mommy." His lower lip quivered as if her sadness unsettled him.

Ray forced a smile and kissed his forehead. "Let's find a treasure, okay?"

Instantly, he brightened, wriggling out of her arms and tugging her hand. "Treasure!"

And just like that, they let the morning become a day of serendipity.

That evening, Ray had an idea.

"Max, how would you like to have a party tonight? We can dance on the patio with our family and friends."

His face lit up. He clapped his hands, bouncing on his feet. Ray couldn't help but scoop him up, swinging him around. He was her life's blood.

"Okay, now I'm going to call Uncle Rihards and Aunt Aria, and you can ask them to come to our party."

She dialed, and when Aria picked up, Max hesitated. She said hello a few times before he finally blurted, "Party!"

Aria chuckled. "Is this Max?"

"I'm Max," he confirmed.

"Are you asking me to come to a party, Max?"

He nodded, even though she couldn't see him. "Party."

Ray took the phone, laughing. "Hey, Aria, how are you and Rihards?"

"We're great! When's the party?"

"Tonight, of course. String lights, music. I'll have the food catered—no one has to lift a finger."

"We're in, all the way!"

"Terrific. I'll have Max call Rachel and Saxton next."

Aria's voice softened. "Are you doing okay, Ray?"

Ray exhaled. "Had an emotional dive earlier, but after Max and I decided to have a party, I feel better."

"You know you can call me anytime, right? Rihards and I are always here for you. You're family. We love you dearly."

Ray's heart swelled. "Thank you, Aria. By the way, how are you feeling? Any more complications?"

"No more bleeding. I'm normalizing. The doctor says it can happen in the first trimester—nothing to worry about. Rihards is over the moon. I think he's convinced we need at least six kids."

Ray laughed. "Have as many as your health allows. Children are gifts from God. And you two are certainly blessed enough to provide for a large family."

"We are. And you and Blake helped us so much when we were just starting out. We wouldn't be where we are without you."

Ray smiled. "We just lived our lives fully and trusted God. That's all."

"That's everything," Aria corrected. "So, what time do we show up to Max's party?"

"Sundown."

"We'll be there."

As Ray hung up the phone, Max grinned and said, "Lights."

"Yes, we will turn on the patio lights. You are a great party planner, little fella!"

The party was perfect.

Everyone arrived as the sun painted the sky in hues of orange and purple, dipping slowly into the ocean. Ray stood outside, taking in the beauty, feeling blessed even in her grief.

She turned and greeted her guests.

"Welcome, everyone! We're so glad you could join us for Max's party!"

Max ran to hug his family. They were all he knew, all he needed.

Rihards swept him up, tossing him playfully in the air. Max squealed with delight. The bond between them was undeniable. Ray watched with a bittersweet ache in her heart—Blake should have been here for this. But she knew, in a way, he was.

Saxton nudged Ray with a grin. "I hear we're having a gourmet dinner catered."

She laughed. "That's right. I tried to choose something for everyone. And for dessert—tiramisu."

Rachel sighed happily. "You always serve us the best food, Ray. Tonight will be wonderful."

The patio was adorned with twinkling string lights. The table was set with care, a vase of red carnations at its center, their fragrance subtly sweet.

They ate, they laughed, they savored.

Max, ever the life of the party, was busy chasing fireflies between bites of food. When the music picked up, he twirled in circles, dancing with unrestrained joy.

Ray watched him, her throat tightening. He was so much like Blake. The thought nearly crushed her.

Rihards noticed. Without a word, he picked Max up. "I'll put his pajamas on and read to him until he falls asleep."

Max reached for Ray. "Kiss, Mommy."

She kissed his soft cheek. "Goodnight, sweetheart."

As Rihards carried Max inside, Ray watched them go. He would make an incredible father.

The evening winded down. Aria tidied the table without being asked, a quiet act of love.

After everyone left, Ray checked on Max. He was fast asleep in her bed. She started to move him but stopped. Why not let him sleep here? He was her comfort, her heart.

She changed into her nightgown and stepped onto the patio one last time.

The full moon glowed, its haze wide and mysterious. A one-of-a-kind moon. Maybe God's way of reminding her that He was personal, intentional.

Music still played softly. The moonflowers shimmered.

Ray closed her eyes and spun in slow circles, letting herself imagine—just for a moment—that Blake was holding her, guiding her in a dance across time and space.

She felt him there.

She walked to the front yard and gazed at the ocean. The moonlight stretched over the water like a path to eternity. Tiny lights danced on the waves like diamonds.

Her mind drifted to the past, to the people she loved and lost. Blake. Byron. Sid. Her parents.

A whispered prayer rose from her lips.

Father, You have blessed me. Max and I will walk out the rest of our lives honoring You. But at times, I feel misplaced in this world. Soothe my soul, sweet Jesus.

She turned back inside and curled up next to Max, holding him close.

Chapter Forty-Three

Joel was a carpenter's son. His mother was a seamstress, and his father remodeled houses. From a young age, he was taught to walk the road less traveled and to fear God. His family was small but close-knit, bound by love, faith, and hard work.

Joel had a younger sister, Jodie, a bright light in his life. But when Jodie was killed in a car accident at the age of fifteen, that light was extinguished. Joel was twenty-one at the time, and in an instant, his world shattered.

His father, once a strong and steady presence, broke under the weight of grief. He quit everything—his work, his faith, his role as a husband and father. He withdrew into himself, leaving Joel's mother to shoulder the burdens of the household alone. For months, Joel listened to his mother's quiet pleas, watched her struggle to keep the family afloat, and felt the deep, aching loss of both his sister and the father he once knew.

One evening, as he sat alone in the silence of their home, Joel made a decision. If his father couldn't be the man of the house, then he would.

With the double-edged sword of grief in his heart, he was determined to build a good life—not just for himself, but for his parents as well. He took on simple jobs and applied what he had learned from his father about restoring old homes. The work was slow at first, but step by step, he learned, improved, and saved.

The first house he bought and remodeled turned a $30,000 profit. That was all the proof he needed. He kept going, buying, restoring, and selling homes. Before long, word spread about the young man with a gift for breathing life into neglected houses. The demand for his work grew, and soon, he hired three men—each eager to learn how to turn hard work into profit. Together, they worked tirelessly, refining their craft, building something greater than just homes. They built a future.

As Joel's business expanded into other cities, he never forgot the values he was raised with. Every employee he hired was taught to work as though they were working for the Lord. Integrity, excellence, and faith became the foundation of his growing enterprise.

Success brought more than financial stability—it allowed Joel to provide for his parents. He remodeled their home, ensuring their comfort, and continued to live with them. It gave him a sense of purpose beyond money—this was his way of repaying them for all they had sacrificed.

And then, love found him.

Sheila was a woman with a heart as big as the world. A devoted teacher, she saw her career not just as a job, but as a ministry. She loved children and longed to be a mother more than anything else.

Joel and Sheila made a formidable team. As his business flourished, they traveled—not just for pleasure, but for purpose. Together, they embarked on mission trips, with Joel teaching carpentry and Sheila teaching children about Christ. They poured themselves into their work, their faith, and their community, becoming pillars of strength and generosity.

But life, as Joel had learned too well, had a way of shifting in an instant.

When Sheila turned fifty, she was diagnosed with ovarian cancer. Four months. That was all the time they had left together.

Joel had already buried his parents in the years before Sheila's death, but losing her—his love, his partner, his anchor—left him utterly alone.

For a while, he tried to press on. He kept working, kept moving forward. But grief is a relentless force, and eventually, it led him down another path. A path that would prove to be the greatest journey of his life.

Joel sold everything—his business, which had grown into a three-state operation, his work vehicles, even his personal truck. He packed a few casual clothes into a backpack and bought a plane ticket.

But before he left—before he stepped into the unknown—he had one last piece of unfinished business.

He walked into a local hospital, met with an administrator, and verified the information he had kept buried in his heart for 32 years.

He was ready.

And so, with nothing but a backpack and a heart full of unanswered prayers, Joel set out on a journey that would take him to the farthest corners of the world—searching, learning, and, perhaps, finding what had been lost for so long.

Chapter Forty-Four

In the evenings, a boy and his dog could often be seen strolling along the shore, their silhouettes etched into every majestic sunset painted by God. The boy, Max, was now eleven, and his faithful companion, Journey, was thirteen—still strong, still by his side.

On this particular evening, as the golden light faded into deep purples and blues, an old man sat on the sand, legs folded, watching the waves roll in. He raised a hand in greeting as Max and Journey passed by.

Max lifted his own hand in response, offering a polite wave. Journey, however, had other ideas. Journey turned and trotted over to the stranger without hesitation.

The old man extended a hand, running it gently over the dog's thick fur. "My, what a handsome fellow you've got there, young man. What's his name?"

"His name is Journey, and I'm Max. We live not too far from here. How about you? Do you live nearby?"

The man nodded. "My name is Joel, and yes, son, I live just a couple of streets over from the beach. I'm new to the area, but I already love it."

Max smiled. "Journey and I walk here every evening. Have you seen us before?"

"This is only the second time. I've just moved into my house a week ago."

Max glanced toward the horizon, then back at the old man. "Mr. Joel, we have to go—Mom will have dinner waiting for us. It was nice to meet you."

Joel nodded with a warm smile. "See you again sometime."

Max had taken only a few steps before turning back to wave once more. Joel lifted his hand in return, his gaze lingering as the boy and his dog disappeared down the shore.

His thoughts drifted to the long, arduous years he had spent searching—searching for meaning, searching for himself, and most of all, searching for his daughter, his own flesh and blood.

His journey had begun with a deep, unshakable longing. Though he had never traveled abroad before, something had drawn him to Brazil, where his father had trained as a pilot for World War II. Standing on the shores of Natal, gazing at the vast Atlantic, he knew he was looking at the same view his father had once beheld as a young man. In that moment, he felt closer to him than ever before.

Joel spent weeks exploring Natal, then took a bus to Rio de Janeiro, where he marveled at waterfalls, ventured into caves, and stood beneath the towering Christ the Redeemer statue. There, he met a group of hikers preparing for a journey through the Tijuca Forest. Without hesitation, he joined them.

The weeks that followed were filled with discovery—new friendships, deep conversations, and nights spent beneath a sky ablaze with stars. One of his fellow travelers, a man named Joe, had retired early but found himself restless, searching for purpose.

After hearing Joel's story of business success, Joe was inspired. He proposed an idea—building a company that would turn its profits into something meaningful, helping people secure modest, dignified homes. Moved by the vision, Joel stayed in Brazil for several years, helping Joe bring the idea to life. He witnessed communities come together, saw families find hope, and realized that this was more than a mission trip—it was the mission of his life.

Before leaving Brazil, Joe invited Joel on a tiger safari in India. Joel, intrigued, agreed. The experience was beyond anything he had imagined—sleeping under the stars, listening to the symphony of the wild, feeling the pulse of nature itself.

During the trip, a local guide approached him with a request. Their village needed safer, more substantial shelters—structures that could withstand both the elements and the threat of tiger attacks. Joel could not refuse. What began as a single project turned into a calling. He stayed, traveling from village to village, teaching, building, helping.

Days turned into years.

When he finally counted the time, he realized he had been a nomad for fifteen years.

Before returning to the States, he picked up a copy of *National Geographic* in an airport. A photograph caught his eye—breathtaking landscapes of Austria. But it was the caption that made his heart stop: *Photos by Gwenyth Ray Belltower.*

His daughter.

For years, he scoured *National Geographic*, searching for any clue that might lead him to her. But information was scarce.

Accepting that the search would take time, he returned to the U.S., settling in a small cabin in Bozeman, Montana. He learned to ski, embraced the brutal winters, and reveled in the promise of summer. For the first time in a long time, he felt something like peace.

Then, one day, everything changed.

While having coffee in a café in Livingston, he noticed an old newspaper clipping on the wall. It was a tribute—years old—honoring one of Montana's most beloved citizens: Gwenyth Ray Belltower. The article credited her with putting Hunza Valley, Pakistan, on the map, calling her work the most stunning photography *National Geographic* had ever published.

Within a week, Joel was gone.

The journey to Hunza Valley was the most challenging of his life, but when he arrived, he understood why his daughter had loved it. The valley was breathtaking, an untouched masterpiece of nature.

For three months, he searched. His first real clue came from a stranger who spoke of a woman named "Ray" who had once lived among them, helping to bring awareness to the valley. The man directed Joel to a treatment center outside of town, where he was told he might find more answers.

With his heart pounding, Joel entered the clinic.

A receptionist greeted him. "Hello, sir. Are you back for treatment, or are you a new patient?"

Joel cleared his throat. "Neither. I'm looking for someone."

"Who are you looking for?"

"My daughter. Gwenyth Ray Belltower. But I believe she goes by Ray." He hesitated before adding, "I don't think she even knows I'm alive."

Recognition flickered in the receptionist's eyes. "Sir, she's a legend here. Just a moment—I'll see if Simon is in medical records today."

A few moments later, a white-haired man approached. "I hear you have questions about Ray Belltower."

Joel extended his hand. "I've been searching for my daughter for more than twenty years. Please—tell me anything you can."

Simon led him into a small conference room, pouring two cups of coffee before settling into a chair. "Ray came to our valley as a young woman, taking photographs for *National Geographic*. She was grieving then—her son had died in an accident. But even in her sorrow, she poured her heart into her work, capturing the soul of this place."

Simon smiled, lost in memory. "She became family to us, especially to me and my son. My wife had been missing for two years at the time, and Ray helped us through our grief. She was selfless. Then, one day, my wife returned. And just like that, Ray was gone."

Joel's breath caught in his throat. "Do you know where she went?"

"The last I knew of Ray's whereabouts was at least ten years ago. She was married to a gentleman named Blake Forsyth and expecting a baby. The two of them lived in Grand Cayman Island."

Joel exhaled slowly. "Then that's where I'll go next."

Simon's voice was warm. "If you find her, tell her we'll never forget her. She was remarkable."

Joel stepped outside, the sun sinking into the horizon, painting the sky in hues of fire and gold.

He closed his eyes and whispered a prayer of gratitude.

For the first time in years, hope was not just a dream. It was real.

And it was leading him home.

Chapter Forty-Five

After feeding Journey his breakfast, Max decided to surprise his mom with breakfast in bed. She had slept later than usual, and he wanted to give her a break.

He carefully brewed her favorite coffee, sliced fresh mango, and warmed up blueberry scones. Once everything was neatly placed on a tray, he added a final touch—a blue vase with a single rose, positioning it securely before carrying the tray to her room.

Tapping gently on her bedroom door, he called out with a smile, "Breakfast served with love!"

Ray opened the door, taking the tray from his hands with a look of pure delight. "Just look at this! My sweet young man, how did you know exactly what I needed this morning?"

Max grinned. "Oh, Mom, I just know that being pampered makes you happy."

"Exactly right," she laughed. "Thank you, Max. Sit with me while I eat like a queen!"

As she settled back into bed, Max sat on the edge, his face suddenly thoughtful.

"Mom, can I ask you something?"

"Of course, honey. What's on your mind?"

"Do you think people can look alike even if they're not related?"

Ray raised an eyebrow. "Yes, I've seen that happen before. Why do you ask?"

"Well... yesterday, when Journey and I were walking on the beach, we met an old man. And something about him reminded me of you."

Ray's breath caught slightly. "Really? How so?"

"I don't know exactly. It wasn't just how he looked—it was the way he talked, his expressions. The moment I saw him, I thought of you."

A strange, unexpected feeling washed over Ray. *Out of the mouth of babes...* Could it be possible? After all these years, after so many silent prayers? She had long since given up on ever seeing her biological father. But Max—Max was more perceptive than most. He had an uncanny way of noticing things others didn't.

Her heart pounded, but she forced a calm smile. "That's interesting, Max."

"Yeah, but we don't have to talk about it anymore. Weren't we supposed to go shopping for my school supplies today?"

Ray exhaled, pushing aside the whirlwind of thoughts. "Yes! Do you have all the lists from your teachers?"

"I do. And hey, when are you going to teach me to drive the mini?"

"In two more years." She smirked. "And when you learn, the mini will be yours."

Max glanced at Journey, his expression softening. "Two years is a long time. Journey might not be with us by then."

Ray reached over, squeezing his hand. "Max, all we have is the time God gives us—a few breaths on this Earth and an eternity of breaths in Heaven. Let's cherish each moment."

Max nodded. "You're right. Okay, I'll take your tray and clean up. Journey and I will be out front, list in hand, ready to go."

Ray kissed his forehead. "You're the best."

That evening, as the vast ocean swallowed the sun, Ray, Max, and Journey played in the shallow water, laughing as the waves lapped at their feet. The air smelled of salt and possibility.

"Hey, Mom," Max called as he skipped a rock across the surface. "I hope we see the old man again today."

Ray chuckled. "Maybe we should think of another name for him."

"What's wrong with 'old man'? He *is* old."

"I know, but when I'm his age, I don't think I'd like being called an old woman."

Max smirked. "I get it. People who are old want to be younger, and people who are young want to be older."

Ray grinned. "Good observation, kiddo."

Just then, Max's eyes lit up. "Mom! I think I see him. Come on, Journey, let's run!"

Ray watched as Max sprinted ahead, Journey bounding beside him, their silhouettes golden in the fading sunlight.

Max skidded to a stop in front of the man sitting on the sand. "Hello, Mr. Joel! I brought my mom to meet you today."

Joel looked up, his breath catching in his throat. In the distance, he saw her. His heart pounded so hard he could barely stand.

She was here.

"Don't you want to meet my mom?" Max asked, puzzled by the man's hesitation.

Joel swallowed hard. "Yes, son. I do." His voice was barely above a whisper.

Ray approached with a warm smile, extending her hand. "Hi, I'm Ray Forsyth. And you are?"

Joel took her hand, holding it just a moment longer than necessary. "I'm Joel Hart."

Ray glanced at Max. "My son was excited to meet you yesterday. He insisted I come along tonight."

"Mom," Max interrupted eagerly, "remember how I told you Mr. Joel looks like you?"

Ray nodded slowly. "Yes, Max. I remember."

Joel cleared his throat. "Well, I'll take that as a compliment."

Max beamed. "Come have dinner with us tonight, Mr. Joel."

Joel hesitated, exhaustion settling in his bones. "I appreciate the invitation, but evenings are tough for me. However..." He smiled. "I do love to cook. How about breakfast at my place tomorrow morning? It's only a couple of blocks from here—314 Brighton Lane."

Max turned to Ray, eyes pleading. "Mom, can we?"

Ray met Joel's gaze, searching for something—an answer, a sign, anything.

"Of course," she said, her voice steady. "What time?"

"Would 8:30 be too early?"

"Not at all."

Joel nodded, his throat tight. "Then I'll see you both in the morning."

As Max and Ray turned to leave, Max called back over his shoulder, "Have a good evening, Mr. Joel!"

Joel stood there long after they disappeared, staring at the spot where Ray had stood.

For the first time in decades, he felt it.

Hope.

Chapter Forty-Six

Joel woke early, savoring the quiet moments before sunrise. He wanted to take his time preparing the breakfast he had in mind. Just the day before, he had carefully selected fresh ingredients—ground pork, Yukon potatoes, an assortment of fruit, and his favorite seasonings.

He began by seasoning the pork, allowing the flavors to meld while he diced fresh fruit, tossing it gently with lemon juice and a dollop of homemade whipped cream. The cream had been whipped the night before, so it was perfectly firm. Next, he mixed flour, baking soda, baking powder, salt, and buttermilk until the batter was smooth and thick. Before placing it on a baking sheet, he folded in finely shredded cheddar cheese and melted butter—his favorite biscuit recipe.

The potatoes were last. He peeled and sliced them into wedges, adding finely chopped sweet onion before sautéing them in olive oil. As the sausage sizzled on the grill, he poured fresh-squeezed orange juice into glasses and brewed a pot of coffee. The table was set for three, and the breakfast nook, bathed in the golden morning light filtering through the palm tree outside, felt warm and welcoming.

When a knock sounded at the front door, Joel's heart pounded. *Oh, Lord, give me the right words. Help me stay at peace.*

He opened the door with a smile. "Please, come in. Breakfast is ready just in time. Have a seat, and I'll serve your plates. I hope you both like fresh-squeezed orange juice. And, Ray, I made coffee just for you—unless Max has taken up drinking coffee, too?"

Max grinned. "I like it sometimes, but only if it's mostly milk and sugar."

Joel chuckled. "I understand, Max. That's exactly how I started drinking coffee."

Ray glanced over the spread and smiled warmly. "This looks like a feast. I'm impressed that you picked and prepared things we love."

"That was my goal," Joel admitted. Then he hesitated before asking, "Max, I usually say a silent prayer before eating, but would you like to bless the food this morning?"

Max nodded. "Yes, sir. Father in heaven, thank You for connecting us with Mr. Joel, and thank You for this food. Please protect us today and keep us in Your will. Amen."

Joel's heart swelled. "Thank you, Max. That was a beautiful blessing."

As they ate, Max grinned between bites. "Mr. Joel, this is amazing! When did you learn to cook like this?"

Joel laughed. "When I was a teenager. But for over twenty years, I spent my time hiking in the mountains and camping, which didn't allow for fancy cooking. Since moving here, I've been working on my skills again."

"I'll say! This is fantastic, isn't it, Mom?"

Ray nodded, savoring the flavors. "It really is. Thank you for inviting us."

Max was the first to finish, and Journey had started to get restless. Ray noticed and smiled. "Max, would you like to take Journey for a walk on the beach?"

"Sure, Mom! Maybe we'll find some treasures since it's still early."

As Max and Journey ran outside, Joel took a deep breath. The moment had come. He reached across the table and gently placed his hand over Ray's.

"Simon in Hunza Valley sends his warmest regards," he said softly.

Ray inhaled sharply. Her voice trembled. "You're my biological father... aren't you?"

Joel's eyes filled with tears. "Yes. I believe so."

For the next two hours, he told her everything—about her mother, about the long, winding path that had led him here, and about the moment he had first seen Max on the beach. Ray listened intently, holding his hand as the past unfolded before her.

When Max and Journey burst back through the door, Max was beaming. "Mom, look what we found! It's a piece of coral shaped exactly like the one Dad found before he..." His voice trailed off.

Ray's face crumpled, and she broke down in uncontrollable sobs.

Max's eyes widened in alarm. "Mom? What's wrong?"

Joel moved instinctively, wrapping his arm around her, pulling her close. He spoke gently to Max. "Son, your mom still grieves for your dad. You were too young to remember, but they made wonderful memories together. Sometimes, when we get an unexpected reminder of someone we've lost, it brings back all the feelings at once. Do you understand?"

Max swallowed hard, his lower lip quivering. "I think so. This little piece of coral reminds Mom of Dad, right?"

Joel nodded, pulling Max close. "That's right. And sometimes, we all need a good cry."

Max sniffled. "Mr. Joel, you sound just like my mom."

Joel smiled. "Well, she's pretty wise, so I take that as a compliment."

Max grinned through his emotions.

Joel hesitated before asking, "Would you like me to walk home with you? That way, I'll know where to visit."

Ray and Max answered at the same time. "Absolutely."

After tidying up the kitchen, the three of them set off toward Ray and Max's cottage. The air was crisp, the sound of the waves steady and soothing.

Each of them walked in thoughtful silence, processing the weight of the day.

For Joel and Ray, the journey had only just begun.

And deep in her heart, Ray wanted to shout, *Yes, Max, you were right—I do look like Joel!*

Chapter Forty-Seven

Ray awoke earlier than usual, the soft glow of dawn just beginning to lighten the sky. The house was quiet, save for the rhythmic sound of waves rolling onto the shore in the distance. She stretched, allowing herself a moment to savor the peacefulness before slipping out of bed.

With gentle steps, she made her way to Max's bedroom door and eased it open just enough to peek inside. He was curled up beneath the covers, his chest rising and falling in a steady rhythm, his face relaxed in deep sleep. There was something about watching her son like this—so at peace, so innocent—that always filled her heart with warmth.

She considered waking him, but then decided against it. School started the next day, and their carefree summer routine would soon be replaced with early mornings, schedules, and responsibilities. Let him sleep a little longer.

Moving to the kitchen, Ray brewed a fresh pot of coffee, inhaling the rich, familiar aroma as it filled the room. She warmed a couple of cinnamon scones in the oven, their scent mingling with the coffee, creating a comforting start to the morning. As she waited, she let Journey outside, watching as the dog trotted into the yard, pausing to sniff the morning air before settling down in his usual spot.

With her coffee in hand and a plate of scones balanced carefully, Ray stepped out onto the patio. The world outside was still wrapped in the quiet hush of early morning, the sky painted in soft pastels of pink and gold. The moonflower blossoms, delicate and pale, were still partially open, as if lingering in the embrace of night.

She sighed, realizing she had forgotten to admire them the night before. These small moments—the ones she used to cherish—had been lost in the rush of emotions and revelations. But now, as she sat in the quiet, she let herself breathe them in again.

Her thoughts drifted to Joel.

He had shared so much about his life—the adventures, the years spent wandering in distant lands, the people he had met along the way. She had listened, fascinated, but she hadn't yet shared much of her own story with him. Tonight, over dinner, she would. After Max was tucked into bed, she would sit with her father and finally tell him about her journey, the struggles, the joys, and everything in between.

It was clear that Max was already enchanted by his grandfather. He had listened with wide eyes to Joel's stories of safaris, of nights spent beneath star-filled skies, of friendships forged in the most unexpected places. Ray had seen the admiration in Max's expression, the way he hung onto every word, the way he already seemed to look up to this man they had only just met.

And Joel... he had come to stay. Ray could feel it in her spirit.

If he had only been seeking closure, he would have left after their reunion. But instead, he had settled in, embraced Max with open arms, and stepped into their lives as if he had always belonged. And maybe, in a way, he had.

Ray thought about his courage, his unwavering faith, his ability to walk into the unknown with nothing but trust in God. It was a strength that ran deep in his character, a quiet but powerful assurance that no matter where he was, he was never truly alone. She had seen that same strength in herself.

She smiled at the realization.

In so many ways, it was like looking in a mirror.

Their eyes were identical—deep, thoughtful, carrying the weight of stories yet untold. Even though his hair had turned white with age, his facial hair still held traces of auburn, a hint of the younger man he once was.

Ray wrapped her hands around her coffee cup, feeling its warmth seep into her fingers. She closed her eyes and breathed deeply.

Looking back on my life now, there is nothing I would change because You, Father, were guiding, carrying, and comforting me every step of the way. You intended a life for me designed to draw me closer to You, to help others see and experience Your love. Please, Father, give Joel a long and healthy life with us—for the sake of Max. He is a beautiful blend of his father, my father, and Your love, sweet Jesus. He is a gift from You, Holy Father, and I am most grateful. I love You, Father.

Tears pricked at her eyes, but they weren't the sorrowful kind. They were full of gratitude, of hope, of a love that stretched far beyond anything she could fully grasp.

Joel's presence was a blessing—one she hadn't expected but welcomed with an open heart. And not just to her, but to her Cayman family as well. He was meant to be here. This was a new beginning, a new journey for them all.

Her mind drifted to an idea—a gathering, a celebration of sorts.

She envisioned the patio alive with laughter, music, and the scent of the ocean breeze. She would play Blake's favorite songs, the ones that still made her heart swell with memories. Max would dance under the open sky, his laughter mingling with the rustling leaves and the swaying moonflower blossoms beneath the full moon.

It would be a night of joy, of love, of honoring the past while embracing the future.

Father in heaven, Your gifts are limitless; Your love is without boundaries. This earthly journey for mankind defines You in every aspect of our preparation for HOME: love and joy, grief and pain, life and death—the mysteries of YOU, Father, our great God.

Ray opened her eyes, exhaling slowly.

Yes, a new journey was beginning.

And she was ready.

About The Author

Laura's books have long delivered on her promise to engage the readers in encounters of grace and healing.

"Where Moonflowers Dance" heralds as Laura's fourth novel and her first offering of light-hearted romance.

Within its pages, you will discover courage & boldness in each character and throughout its entirety, you'll be held in the grip of enchanting adventures, suspenseful engagements, and tales of glorious hope.

"Where Moonflowers Dance" will heighten your desire to experience nature, community, and our majestic Creator's full goodness.

Laura serves as a caregiver to her husband and lives in Cornelius, NC. She enjoys serving in her community church and relaxes by writing at night.

Made in the USA
Middletown, DE
12 October 2025